Discovery

SISTERHOOD CHRONICLES 2

ANITA DAVIS

ISBN-10: 1-946721-01-8
ISBN-13: 978-1-946721-01-3

Books may be purchased in quantity by contacting the author Anita Davis.:
Set Apart Publishing
PO Box 39229
Chicago, IL 60659
or by email at authoranitadavis@gmail.com

ACKNOWLEDGMENTS

To my mother who always gives interesting and truthful feedback of my writing. Thank you, girl.

To my sorority sister, Latrease, aka Choctaw, I love you and your dedication to reading this work quick and in a hurry and giving me invaluable feedback. Thank you.

To my cousin, Nay Nay, thank you for reading this and making me laugh with your noted feedback. You showed me how readers would possibly interact with the characters in the book. Thank you.

Thank you to my friend, Gabrielle Marcelle for your continued support of my writing career.

To my two wonderful editors on this project, Janelle Smith Toussant and Akilah Crossland, I know I'm stubborn, but you ladies still deal with me in spite of. ***inserts smile here***

Thank you to everyone else who helped me to prepare this book for someone other than myself.

Thank you to all the readers who read the first book in this series, "Underneath It All", and noted how you couldn't wait to read the next book. Your excitement for this series motivated me to get this book to you as soon as possible. I hope you enjoy "Discovery".

"Though no one can go back and make a brand new start, anyone can start from now and make a brand new ending." ~*Carl Bard*.

Prologue

He rolled over from off top of her after having pleased himself with her for the third time since he'd been there that eve. He lay on his back taking deep breaths trying to lower his heart rate. He looked over at her to see that guilty, yet pensive look she held on her face after every time they had sex. He knew what was coming next.

She rolled on her side and draped her arm across his chest as she nestled under his arm soaking in his zesty scent that now only mingled with hers once a week. Her long eyelashes batted as she looked up at him. "So you can stay tonight right?" She lightly traced circles around his nipples with her fingertips.

He kissed her forehead. "You know I can't stay." He hoped that would be the end of that conversation.

Pouting with puppy dog sadness in her eyes, she jumped up and on top of him staring at him. "But why not?"

"I just can't."

She slapped his chest hard. "Is it really over between you two? Don't lie to me."

"Yes, it is." He smiled sitting up as he gathered her hands and wrapped them around his neck. "You know I like it when you're on top." He spoke between the light kisses he placed on her neck. "Let's do it again." He moaned as he gripped her butt trying to position her perfectly on top of him.

The screen lit up on his phone and it vibrated as it rested on the nightstand next to the bed. He ignored it and continued kissing her.

Annoyed with the constant vibrating of his phone from calls and texts at that time of the night, she mustered up enough resolve to push him back from her. He fell back allowing his head to hit the pillow. He folded his arms behind his head. "I don't know why you resist me at times, you know you're going to give in." He smirked as he gyrated his pelvis under her.

Her nostrils flared as she folded her arms across her chest. "Why won't you answer your phone? Obviously someone is trying to get in contact with you."

"I don't care who it is. All I care about is you right now. So come on and let's do it one more time before I leave." He tried to sit up again to kiss her, but she pushed him back down.

"Leave? Why do you have to leave? You never stay."

"I told you it's easier to leave for work from my house than from all the way out here." He sighed in frustration.

Her eyes narrowed in on him. She was tired of distance being his reason he never spent the night with her. "I've tried to be patient with you, but that excuse is getting played out. Do you really live alone now?"

"Yes. I pay $850 a month for a one bedroom apartment."

"So is your divorce final?"

He sighed. "No, not yet."

"Have you even started the process?"

"No Pam, it's not that simple."

"It's not that simple? It's over with her, and you love me right?"

His phone continued to vibrate on the night stand.

He let out an exasperated sigh. "Yes Pam." He rubbed his face in frustration.

"So then it is simple. Finalize your divorce so that we can get married soon."

His eyes widened. His phone continued to vibrate on the night stand.

"Why are you looking at me like that? You do still wanna marry me right?"

"Yes, bae." He huffed as he gently pushed her off of him and got out of the bed. He stretched his long, lean, yet muscular body as he stood on the side of the bed. He headed to the bathroom with her on his heels.

His phone was now vibrating in her hand as he stood over the toilet relieving himself. She stood in the doorway staring from him to his phone. "Why is she calling you right now?"

He looked over to see Pam holding his lit phone wagging it at him. His eyebrows furrowed. "Why do you have my phone?"

Pam ignored his question to ask her own. "I see she's been calling you nonstop for the past twenty minutes. Why?"

He adjusted himself in his boxers and turned to her reaching for his phone.

She jumped back from him with his phone behind her back.

"Give me my phone Pam."

"Not until you answer me. If you all aren't together anymore and you have your own place, why is she calling you this time of the night?"

"I don't know, maybe it has something to do with my kids."

Pam gasped. "Kids? You have kids?"

"Yes, I have kids. Now give me my phone so I can make sure they're okay."

Since his phone was identical to hers, Pam knew what she was doing when she slid the green button to the right on his vibrating screen. She ran across the room as she put the phone up to her ear. "Hello."

"Who the hell is this?" The woman on the other end of the phone demanded an answer.

"Who is this?" Pam shot back.

"This is the wife of the man's phone you're on. Where is my husband?"

"Why do you care?" Pam snapped growing tired of the woman on the other end.

"I don't have to answer you, but I will just in case you don't know and didn't hear me, he's married. I hope to God you ain't one of them thirsty side chicks that's known all along that he's married but still creeping with him."

The more she listened to his wife, the more frustrated she became with herself and with Steve.

"Are you listening?" His wife didn't even let Pam answer her before she continued on, "he was supposed to be playing his weekly pickup game with his home boys at the gym and they were gonna do some strength training after that, but since it's twelve at night, none of his friends can vouch for where he is, and he hasn't been answering his phone. Would you please tell his trifling tail that I'm in the emergency room at Rush hospital with his son, Steve Jr." The woman hung up the phone.

Pam had the phone on speaker the whole time making Steve privy to every word his wife said. His words were caught in his throat as he watched the tears spill from Pam's eyes. He knew she really was a good woman, a little naive if you asked him, but a good woman with a good heart nonetheless. He never wanted the affair to go on as long as it had been, but the more time he spent with her, granted he couldn't give her much of his time, the more he wanted to be with her. However, there was only so much time he could spend with her as a married man.

The sound of his phone breaking against the wall brought him back into the present. Pam's hand was still in the air from having thrown his phone at him, but with her poor aim, it hit the wall.

"Kids? You have kids? You have a junior?" She clutched her chest trying to assuage the pain in her chest. She knew enough medically to know that she wasn't exhibiting signs of a heart attack, but rather heartbreak.

"Pam, you've known for a while that I'm married." Steve looked at her as he started gathering his clothes from the floor.

"Aaahhh! I hate you." The conversation with his wife infuriated her beyond her normally calm behavior. She charged at him. "Why do you keep lying to me?"

Steve grabbed Pam forcing her hands to her side as he looked into her eyes searching for the docile woman he enjoyed spending time with. When he no longer saw her in Pam he became worried.

"I hate you. I didn't know you were married at first. I certainly didn't know you had kids. I've only stayed with you because you told me it was over with her."

"It is baby." He pulled her in closer to him trying to kiss her but she used all of her might to break free of his hold.

"No, it's not. She just said you were supposed to be coming home to her tonight after your game. So that's what I am? A game to you?"

"No." He pulled his shirt over his head and slipped into his boots. "You're so much more to me than that." He zipped his pants up and put on his jacket.

"I can't be anything to you with all of this lying you've been doing since day one."

"Look, my phone is broke now. I can't even call to check up on my son. I have to go. We'll talk about this later."

"Later? There is no later. I hate you. I never wanna see you again" She followed him through her house pounding on his back as he headed to the door. "I hate you. I don't ever wanna see you again." She screamed as she slammed the door behind him.

.

1

One year later

Pam sat alone in the restaurant waiting on the rest of the sisterhood. She smiled thinking about how Renee and Kim's mother, Mrs. Williams, donned that name on them before they started their first year of college. She remembered how they all stood on the steps outside of their dormitory when Mrs. Williams demanded their attention and said, "Ladies, you all are a sisterhood. I expect you to stick together and continue to look out for one another as you have since middle school. You hear me?" They liked the term 'sisterhood' referring to the bond they shared with one another. The idea of calling themselves the sisterhood stuck with them from that point on.

People around Pam smiled at her, merely acknowledging her presence with pleasantry on their faces, while others seemed to be oblivious to her existence.

She looked over at one woman cooing at her husband and she could've sworn that the woman snarled at her. She didn't even know the woman, but she wondered if the woman knew what she had done.

Pam turned her attention back to her table and shook her head thinking about how she had been avoiding her best friends, Kim, Monica, and Renee. It had been a little over a year since they all had been in a room together; not since Monica had given birth to her twins.

Pam tried not to be so condemning of herself, but with what she had done, misery engulfed her.

At first, she wasn't able to visit with the sisterhood as often as they used to hang out together because of her work and school schedule. Being a teacher was very time consuming, and the added stress of pursuing her masters while holding down a full-time job left her without time for any recreational activities; well that was until *he* came along.

Pam looked up again from her table to see her friends across the street at the light waiting to cross Madison Ave. She hoped that he wouldn't be up for discussion.

While she was waiting for them to enter the restaurant, her mind replayed when she first met him. She managed to sneak in conversations with her friends about him but the closer the two got, the less time she had to talk to them. She would have loved nothing more than to introduce him to her friends, but once she found out the secret he was keeping from her, she wouldn't dare introduce him to her friends. When she first found out about it she went on and on to herself how she would leave him immediately, but he had a hold of her heart and she pretty much had to pry it out of his hands to get away from him.

She looked up as she saw the rest of the sisterhood make their entrance into the restaurant. Pam sat up straight, cleared her throat, and tried to wipe away any of the guilt and sadness that may have laced her face.

Customers around the room briefly stared at the quartet as they embraced one another with hugs and kisses before they took their seats.

Pam knew she needed to guide the conversation rather than let them choose a topic, which would most likely be her love life, or lack thereof, so she spoke up first. "Oh I'm so glad I'm finally done with school." Pam breathed a sigh of relief as she and the others scooted into their booth.

"Girl, I know you are. It was taking up all of your time." Renee said.

"Congratulations." Monica smiled.

"Nah, that wasn't the only thing taking up all of her time, she has a man too. The man that we've never met," Kim said shaking her head. "I can't believe you're dating someone we've never met."

Pam sat there quietly averting eye contact with her friends.

"What's wrong? Why are you acting so nervous and all? We're only talking about the love of your life as you made him out to be, you know, the one that kept you from us." Monica pursed her lips.

"No ladies, it wasn't him that kept me so busy and away from you all. It was all of the work that I had to do for my masters and what I had to do at work. Between classes and my teaching responsibilities, I was honestly too busy to hang out with you all." Pam hoped they wouldn't bring him up again.

"But you hung out with him." Kim cocked her head at Pam.

"Every time we called you to hang out, you ditched us and our plans because you were waiting to see him. You never mentioned having to do work for school or grade any of your students' papers." With raised eyebrows, Kim studied Pam.

Pam smiled at the mention of her students. She really did love to teach. "Yeah, yeah, yeah, I was in love, or at least I thought I was." Pam mumbled the last part to herself.

Kim's combative nature rose. She was ready to delve more into what Pam mumbled. "What was that you said?" Her round eyes widened as she spoke.

"Nothing, I was simply saying that yes my time was filled, but that's over now, so you all don't have to worry about him taking up my time. He's old news, I'm done with him."

"What? Wait. Back it up. Press rewind. You said it's over with him?" Kim said.

"Yes, that's what I said."

"But we never got the chance to meet him." Renee joined in on the interrogation.

"Enough about me ladies, what about you all?" Pam sighed.

"Enough about you? You've told us nothing about you." Kim playfully snarled at Pam. "Oh, we're just getting started."

"No, we're not." Pam rolled her eyes.

"Yes, we are." Kim slammed her hand down on the table as if she had the final say so of how the conversation would go.

They laughed before Renee spoke up. "Monica was once in the hot seat and we interrogated her for quite some time before her and Keith got married and had the twins. Now, it's your turn."

"My turn, why my turn?" Pam put her hand over her chest as she spoke.

"Because you went off and had a world wind affair with a man we never met." Renee smiled.

"Affair? Why'd you have to say that?" Pam's palms grew clammy.

"Girl, that's only a saying. Would you have preferred if she called it a romance?" Kim furrowed her eyebrows at Pam.

"I'd prefer if you all call it nothing. Because that's what it was, nothing."

Monica knew what it was like to be the center of the women's attention and wanted to stay out of the interrogation of Pam as best as she could, but she couldn't help herself any longer. "Jeesh, Pam, you're squeezing that glass of water so tight, it looks like it's about to break."

Pam looked down to realize how tight of a grip she had on the glass. She let it go and flexed her knuckles trying to relieve some of the tension that had built up in her since the ladies had started questioning her.

Monica, Kim, and Renee shared a "we'll get to the bottom of this soon enough look" before Kim decided to be the spokesperson for the trio.

"Well, since you're being so tight-lipped about it, we'll leave it alone for now, but remember, secrets don't last long in this sisterhood." Kim signaled for the waitress to come to the table seeing as though they had silently ushered her away when they thought Pam was going to clue them in on her mystery man; they didn't want any interruptions during the debriefing.

The waitress took their orders and left the table allowing them to continue to grill one another.

"So, since we've agreed to take the spotlight off Pam for now, how about we shine it on you Monica." Kim said.

Pam exhaled and relaxed in her chair.

"Who, lil' ole' me?" Monica smiled pointing at herself.

"Yes, lil' ole' you." Kim responded and they all laughed.

"Monica, you have done such a great job with getting the weight back off after you had the twins, not that you wouldn't look great at any size." Renee said.

"Thanks, but girl you know I had to. After all that I had to go through to get the weight off the first time around and feel good about myself, I didn't want to let years go by still looking like I'm pregnant."

"That would be okay. You could tell people it's baby fat." Kim said.

"No, some honest person would come along and tell me 'that's just fat baby.' "

"You're so silly." Pam said.

"Seriously, yes, along my weight loss journey I learned to love the inside of me which led me to see my outside was just as beautiful."

They all smiled recounting Monica's journey to self-love.

"But, I must admit that I love the naked me when I'm fit and I know Keith does too." Monica almost choked on a piece of gum laughing so hard at herself.

"Ewww!" Pam laughed.

"T-M-I. I don't want to hear about you and my brother's sexcapades." Renee scrunched her nose as she spoke.

Monica buckled over with laughter enjoying watching Keith's sisters cringe every time she mentioned how much she enjoyed being intimate with her husband.

"We know he loves you naked, skinny, tall, small, any way you are, he just loves you. Always has and always will." Kim said.

"Speaking of Keith, how is he doing?" Pam asked.

"You would know if you came around, called more often." Kim sucked her teeth and rolled her eyes.

"Whatever." Pam rolled her eyes at Kim.

They held each other's stare before they burst into laughter.

Monica spoke up amidst the laughter. "Keith is doing great and is so helpful with the twins. He's such a great dad and a great husband too." Monica winked and licked her lips.

"Again, T-M-I," Renee said.

"Enough about me, let's have Renee fill you in on her life since you refuse to get back in the hot seat." Monica looked at Pam.

"Thank you very much." Pam nodded her head as she spoke.

"Well-"

The waitress returned to the table with the ladies food and placed each of their meals in front of them. They thanked her and she left the table again.

Kim picked up her fork ready to dig into her catfish, collard greens, macaroni and cheese, sweet potatoes, and cornbread when Renee stuck her in the hand with a fork.

"Ouch! Why'd you do that?" Kim asked.

"Because you know we say grace before we eat." Renee stared at Kim.

"I said it in my head before the food came. I can't help that you ordered that bland salad. If you had what I'm about to tear into, you'd be ready to smash it ASAP too." Kim stuck out her tongue.

The other ladies struggled to contain their laughter as they bowed their heads and held hands to pray.

Monica began to pray. "Dear God, we thank you for blessing this food, the hands that prepared it-"

Loud munching could be heard at their table.

Renee opened one of her eyes to spy where the sound was coming from to find Kim chewing her food. Renee shook her head and closed her eyes again as she tuned back into the prayer.

"…and God we thank you for our friendship lasting through time. And for blessing us with the wisdom to be there for one another in good and bad times. Straighten out whatever may be crooked in our lives…"

My heart. A tear fell from Pam's eye.

Monica continued praying and they ended it by all saying "amen" together. They looked up at Kim as she repeated saying "amen" with a mouth full of food.

Their eyes shifted to her plate to see that over a fourth of her food was gone.

She looked up at them, "What? That was a loooong prayer, Monica."

"But it was a necessary prayer," Renee said.

"And it was necessary for me to eat. I said I was starving." She stuck another forkful of sweet potatoes in her mouth.

Pam, Renee, and Monica shook their heads as they laughed at Kim.

The other ladies began to dig into their food.

"Okay Renee, give up the goods, what's new with you?" Pam said.

"There's not that much to tell about me right now. I keep busy being a social worker and working with the singles' and children's ministries at church." Renee smiled and ate more of her salad.

"See how much action you've missed in Renee's life, Pam." Kim laughed at herself before the others joined in.

"Oh whatever." Renee rolled her eyes at Kim. She laughed as she put her cup to her mouth.

"Okay, so now that you're caught up with everyone else, let's get back to the mystery man." Kim rubbed her hands together as she smirked at Pam.

Pam's breathing became uneven. She fanned herself. "No, I'm not up for discussion, but you can be. What have you been up to?" Pam gulped her ice water down.

Kim side-eyed Pam. "That's okay missy. You must've forgotten that we'll be working at the same elementary school now, I'll be seeing you daily, I *will* find out about him soon enough."

Kim let out a menacing laugh that made the rest of them look at her with raised eyebrows. "Well, there's nothing new about me seeing as though being fabulous has always been a hobby of mine." She laughed while the others shook their heads at her. "No seriously, I'm glad we'll be working in the same building together, it means I get to see you more. I've missed you." Kim patted Pam's hand.

"What, Kim being sentimental and all, Jesus must be returning soon." Monica said looking at Renee and then to Pam.

"Oh shut up Monica." Kim rolled her eyes.

"Okay, so you won't fill us in on this man, but can you at least tell us why you've decided to move into the city and work in it too? You loved your school and house in the suburbs so much." Monica said.

Pam cleared her throat. Her mind raced with what to share that wouldn't open the door to a discussion of him. "Well, yes I loved working and living in the suburbs, but with some of the courses and research I was doing while getting my masters, I was reminded of why I wanted to teach in the first place. I wanted kids of color to see someone like them empowering them."

"Okay, so why the frown if you're happy to work in the city now?" Renee said.

"Because, being a Chicago Public School teacher means that I have to live in the city limits."

"Ok." Monica said.

"And since I had to move back in the city, I wanted to get the condo I've always dreamed of."

"Okay, so did you find one you like?" Kim said.

"Yes."

"Okay, so why are you still frowning silly?" Monica said.

"Because it's still in its developmental stages, my house in the burbs already sold, so I'll have to live with my parents until my place is ready."

"Oh." Kim, Renee, and Monica said at the same time knowledgeable of Pam's wary feelings of her mother.

Pam laughed. "Now you get why I was frowning." Pam rubbed her forehead trying to massage away the headache that seemed to be forming.

"Well, I happen to like your mother." Kim said.

"Me too." Renee and Monica laughed as they said it at the same time.

"Yeah, because she's not yours."

"She's not bad though." Kim said.

"But she is very opinionated. She's bearable when we're not under the same roof and she doesn't know every detail of my life. But since I know how it was growing up under her roof, I am so not ready to get back under it. Living with her again and seeing me go to and fro, I feel like she'll have more material of my life to criticize."

"Well, how long will it be before your place is done? And you know if you need to you can stay with one of us." Renee said.

"Speak for yourself." Kim stared down Renee.

"They say around Christmas, and whatever Kim." Pam rolled her eyes at Kim and then laughed.

"Oh, you should be fine then, that's like three months or so." Kim said.

"I guess, and I knew if I really needed to, you all," she stuck her tongue out at Kim, "would've welcomed me into your homes. But I wouldn't dare intrude on you all like that, especially not Monica and Keith and the twins."

"Well, if you feel you can't make it through these next months living with your parents, you can stay with me, but I think you'll be fine," Renee said.

"Thanks." Pam smiled at Renee.

"Well, you're my girl and all, but working together and living together might be a little bit too much for me. You know how I am." Kim smiled cunningly and dabbed at the corners of her mouth.

"Thanks ladies, and yes Kim, I know how you can be and how you need your privacy, that's why I didn't dare ask you." Pam poked her bottom lip out and turned her sad-looking face towards Kim.

"Oh, whatever. You know I would let you in if you needed to." Kim said.

They all laughed.

"Well ladies, I've really enjoyed myself, but I really do miss the twins and can't wait to get back to them and Keith." Monica winked.

"There you go again with the TMI about my brother." Kim feigned being nauseous as she covered her mouth.

They signaled for the waitress to bring them the check.

They all began reaching for their wallets.

"No ladies, dinner is on me." Pam said.

"Say what?" Kim cocked her head at Pam.

"Yeah, a little makeup for not having seen you all in so long. I'm sorry." Pam smiled at them.

"Well, I accept." Kim put her wallet back in her purse.

"You don't have to Pam. We understand you were busy."

"No we don't Monica, and that's why we can let her pay for dinner." Kim laughed.

"Monica, I got this." Pam gave the waitress her credit card and rushed the girl to leave the table before the women tried to split the bill.

"Well, since you have the bill, I'mma head on out. I have a date, and don't even bother to ask with who, you know he's temporary." Kim threw her purse on her shoulder.

The other three ladies shook their heads as Kim kissed them on their cheeks and gathered her purse.

"Wait sis, I'll walk out with you." Renee said.

Renee kissed Monica and Pam on their cheeks and caught up with Kim before she exited the restaurant.

"You headed out too, right?" Pam asked Monica.

"Yeah, but you look so despondent again. Wanna talk about it?" Monica looked over at Pam.

"Oh, nothing is wrong with me. I was just in deep thought."

"Pam, if you really need to talk about it, I can call Keith and tell him I'll be a little late getting home."

"Oh no, I won't keep you out any longer."

Monica paused for a second waiting to see if Pam would give in to sharing why she was so sad, but when Pam didn't, she continued speaking, "I guess. Well, let's go."

Still deep in thought, Pam followed Monica out of the door wishing she could either erase her recent past or fast forward years ahead to where her past didn't affect her the way it had been lately.

2

Pam scurried into Jensen Academy with her hands filled with bags full of supplies and her mother dragging behind her complaining.

"Pam, you can't do everything in one day, so what was the purpose of having to bring in all of these bags today?"

"Ma, even if I don't get as much done as I want to today, I still will have these things in my room when I do need them..." She let her words trail off as her mind tried to wrap itself around all that she had to do to prepare for the first day of school.

She was in such a rush to get to the main office, sign in, and then to her classroom that she didn't notice the handsome man posted behind the desk. However, Pam's purpose for being at the school didn't compare to her mother's desire to learn more about the aesthetically pleasing man behind the desk clad in a baby blue Ralph Lauren polo shirt that showcased the bulging muscles of his toned upper body.

As Pam stood in the main office chatting with Ms. Noble, the school's secretary, the one-sided conversation behind her became increasingly louder.

"Pam, you should marry him. Look at him over there, he is so handsome with those big black gorgeous eyes, oh yeah. Make him my son-in-law. He's a better catch than that last one who was-"

"Ma." She spoke loud enough to shut her mother up but spoken softly enough as to not disturb the man sitting behind the desk who seemed unaware of the gawking older woman making a scene.

"Let's go upstairs now. That's why I didn't want to bring you here with me. I have to work with these people and I don't need you showing your true colors and causing drama in my workplace."

"Aw girl hush." Her mother let the words escape from her mouth as they walked up the stairs to Pam's classroom. "I didn't beg you to come up here, you asked me for my help. If you wouldn't have ostracized your friends over the past year, then maybe they would've been willing to help you."

"Ma, nothing is wrong with my friendship with the girls, they simply couldn't help me because they are all working women too. They're unavailable right now." Pam rolled her eyes knowing her mother couldn't see them.

"Well doesn't Kim work at this school? Why couldn't she help you?" Eilene said, fanning herself trying to cool down.

"Yes she does, but she's busy getting her room together too, so she can't help me."

"Tuh, seems to me with all of the schooling y'all have between y'all, the two of you would have enough sense to work together to help each other and do one room at a time and leave out us non-teaching folks."

Pam shook her head in angst. "Mom, we each have too much to do in our own rooms to be in one another's."

"If you say so."

Pam hated it, but she needed her mother's help that day. The spacious storage closet in the classroom had to be organized. Bulletin boards needed to be put up. The whole classroom needed to be sanitized, but she didn't know how much more of her mother she could endure if her mother continued berating her. Luckily for her, her mother was too tired and out of breath by the time they reached the third floor to focus on anything other than getting to the nearest seat to catch her breath and to sip on some of her ice-cold water bottle.

They entered the room and Pam smiled appreciating how much bigger the classrooms were in the city than they were in the suburbs. She looked over to the outdated LCD projector on a desk near the classroom door. She frowned as she was reminded of how she lost the vast technology access she had become accustomed to having for her and her students. She realized she would have to be creative in tweaking lesson plans she had developed that required certain technology.

Eilene made her way into the classroom. She detested how Pam poured herself into her work life while her love life was in shambles. "All you wanna do is work, you need to be thinking about getting a man, your *own* man and giving me a grandchild at your expense before I die."

"Ma, I'm only thirty-two and you're in your mid-fifties. We have plenty of time to worry about me getting a *husband* and then having kids." Pam let the husband part linger in the air. *If You ever bless me Lord with one of my own after what I did.*

"Yeah, a husband, just not someone else's husband." Eilene smacked her lips and headed over to open a window to catch a fresh wind of air.

Pam was so frustrated with herself for accidentally letting the details of her relationship with *him* slip out one day during a conversation with her mother. She wished her mother had a filter or an off button when it came to what she thought was best for Pam. She took a deep breath knowing it was best if she kept her mouth closed at that time. If she opened it, she feared she would only say something disrespectful to her mother and she would have to apologize for it later.

They worked tirelessly for the next few hours preparing the room for the first day of school.

Their time in the classroom had come to an end for the day. As they were leaving, Pam managed to suppress her bitterness of her recent failed relationship and the tension between her and her mother for the time being. She felt excited about the start of the new school year and a new chapter in her life.

3

"Girl, you would think that after four years of spending our money at Howard, a master's degree in education, and then years of teaching out in Skokie that she would have enough sense not to have to move back in here with us."

"Aw hush, Eilene, leave that girl alone. You should be proud of her and all that she has accomplished. She can't help that her new district's living policy requires her to live in the city limits. The fact that her condo isn't even built yet and won't be ready for months ain't her fault either." Paula, Eilene's best friend spoke.

"Puh-lease. If she would make smarter decisions, she wouldn't need to live here with us. I know we raised her better than what she shows at times. For one, who spends so much money on a condo that's not even built?"

Paula laughed before she spoke. "Well, the girl said she wanted to live in that exact neighborhood since she had to move back in the city."

"We raised her in the city without any trouble."

"Yes, but this is a nice neighborhood full of older people and no available houses. She's young. I suspect she wanted to live closer to downtown Chicago. You know, where there's always something for her to get into, you know, explore." Paula snapped her fingers and danced in her chair.

Eilene shook her head at Paula's attempt to dance. "Explore? She needs to explore a man's life background before she falls in love with him. Melvin and I tried our best to raise her the right way, but she still managed to make such a foolish mistake." Eilene shook her head as she continued to peel potatoes.

"Lene, what are you talking about?"

Eilene dropped the knife and potato she held. She braced herself on the counter top as she looked at her friend of forty years. "Girl you can't tell nobody, because I surely don't want anyone to know, but that daughter of mine, that goddaughter of yours, had the nerve to fall in love with a married man."

Paula grabbed her stomach and clasped her mouth. "Shut yo' mouth. No she didn't. Not my sweet little Pam."

"Sweet my foot. Yes she did, and do you know that when she found out that he was married, she didn't end it with him right away."

Paula sat silent clinging on to every word Eilene was saying.

"Girl yes. It took her a minute to break it off with him." Eilene shook her head as she started back peeling her potatoes.

"I hear what you're saying, but I don't believe it. Not Pam. Not focused and determined Pam."

"Yes, that Pam. I guess she was determined to have a man despite him being someone else's. She said she was so deep in love with him and she knew that it wasn't right, but he kept telling her that it was over with his wife. She's a fool I tell ya. She stayed with him thinking he was really done with his wife. I guess when she realized that she still was the side chick as the young folks say, she left him." Eilene shook her head.

"Wow."

"Wow ain't it. She shouldn't have been sexing him and they weren't married. And she shole should've left him alone the minute she found out he was a married man. Melvin and I thought we raised three good kids. You've known them since they were born. My boys Melvin Jr. and Eric are great, but my baby Pam," Eilene shook her head. "I don't get her. I kind of figured she might be naïve when it comes to boys because of the way her father and I sheltered her from them when she was growing up, but I didn't know she would be flat out dumb when it came to men."

"Oh Eilene, hush. That girl ain't dumb. Maybe she was really lonely and blind to who he really was."

"Lonely? She has me, her father, her brothers and their wives and kids, plus her friends that she grew up with, the Sisterhood as she calls them. She ain't got no business being lonely." Eilene laughed adding her potatoes to the pot on the stove.

"Naw, you know for a woman, being around a woman ain't the same as being around a man."

"Yeah, that may be true, but that woman has to be smart enough not to be around a man that belongs to another woman "

Pam stood at the kitchen door listening to her mom Eilene confide in her godmother Paula about her affair and the fact she was living back at home with them. Her dad didn't have a problem with her temporary living arrangements, so she didn't understand why her mom did.

She always heard stories or saw talk shows where people bashed sons for still living at home with their parents past a certain age, but she never knew that was the case for daughters. Wanting to derail her mother's conversation, she entered the kitchen.

"Hi Auntie Paula." Pam sang as she went to the dish rack to grab a cup.

"Hi Pammie, how are you doing today?"

"She would be doing a lot better if she used her head instead of her hormones."

"Momma, please stop being so dramatic. I know I made a mistake, but you don't have to keep throwing it in my face."

"Well, I ain't gon' do it behind your back. Open rebuke is good for you."

Pam stood silent brooding. She wanted to let her mother have a good tongue lashing at times, but she knew better than that. She took a big gulp of her water trying to calm herself down. "Don't worry momma, as soon as my place is done I'll be out of your hair."

"You're not in my hair, you're in my house. I raised you better than being somebody's fool. I don't understand why you didn't do your homework on him. I don't care how charming he may have been, you shouldn't have been his fool. Ain't no man worth your salvation. Had you took the time to get to know him, brought him here to meet us, I would've been able to judge his character. That's why your brothers' marriages have lasted as long as they have. I met their wives, assessed their characters, and confirmed to both of my sons that each of their women were a great catch."

"Eilene, be quiet. You aren't always right. Sometimes you have to let kids learn from their own mistakes."

"Kids? She ain't a kid. She's thirty-two years old."

"I know that momma, you remind me of my age and what I did every day." Pam took a deep breath. "I wish you would be here to comfort me while I'm learning from my mistakes instead of condemning me. You make me feel like I'm not wanted here." Pam stormed out, but her exit wasn't as productive as she would've liked it to be because she ended up in her room in her parents' house.

4

Vance Sutherland was excited to enter his third year as the principal of Jensen Academy. Although he didn't inherit a challenging school to begin with, under his tutelage, the school had grown tremendously academically. The teachers and students had come to love the culture he helped to foster at the school.

Although his job did require a lot of his time, he was still able to keep up his "work hard, play harder" motto on the weekends that he had developed for himself over the years.

Playing hard is exactly what he did. Almost every Friday he would hang out with his friends. Their friendship dated back to elementary school. They were always there for one another and vowed to do that no matter what life brought their way.

Friday nights were their chances to frequent social gatherings to chill with one another and to scout their potential life mates. Some of them, like Anthony and Marcus, had already found their soul mates, while Darius and Vance hadn't been so fortunate in that department of life.

Vance was what some would call a classic man; a sophisticated style of his own. The sound of jazz filled his house as he took his time grooming himself before he would head out with the fellas. He would leave the shower with nothing to cover his naked body since he lived alone on the south side of Chicago. He stood six feet five inches tall. Every inch of him had been sculpted to perfection. From his solid calves to his precisely cut hamstrings, to his washboard abs to his chiseled chest that gave way to the extensions of his massively muscular biceps and triceps. His Adonis physique could be attributed to his daily workout regimen. However, his mother and father were to thank for his smooth chocolate Hershey's kisses colored skin.

He allowed his neat mustache and goatee to frame his full lips and his hair was cut low in waves atop his head. While any woman would marvel at his stature and body, they would be sure to get lost in his eyes, which defined him. They were of an almond shape and the irises of his eyes at times appeared to be as black as onyx. They seemed to speak to a woman's soul long before he ever opened his mouth to talk. When he did speak, his use of the English language was guaranteed to make any woman weak in the knees longing to have more time to hear his deep sultry masculine voice.

Even with Vance's looks, charm, and financial standing, there was still something lacking in his life.

5

After the time spent putting her classroom together and calming herself down after another run-in with her mother, the only thing Pam wanted to do was relax in her own bed at her own house; but her old bed in her parents' house would be her only comfort in the meantime.

Pam exited the bathroom after soaking in the tub. Her Snickers candy bar complexion glistened under the pale moonlight peeking through the curtains.

It was a Saturday night and she laid in the bed with the lights off, but a lavender scented candle flickered on the nightstand next to her. Neo-soul music played softly in the background. Her slanted brown eyes adjusted to the lighting in the room. She needed to clear her mind before the school year officially started that Monday. She tried and tried to find a comfortable spot in that moment mentally, but only thoughts and memories of Steve flashed across her mind disturbing her serenity. She didn't wear her usual bright and beautiful smile that night; it had been dimmed by the events of her recent past and her current living situation.

This time last year she was so in love and enjoying all of her time spent with him. Thinking back, she never considered herself to be a gullible woman when it came to men, but clearly after Steve, she had to reassess whether or not she knew how to identify the right man for her.

She remembered meeting him at a grocery store one night she had to make a run to get some treats for her students the next day. She found herself in the produce section getting fruits and vegetables to replenish her supply running low at home.

After getting her produce, she headed to the dairy section and spotted him. She immediately admired him for the handsome man he was, but turned away trying to remember whether or not she actually had milk at home. She never was the type to approach a man. She figured if one was ever interested in her then he would make it his business to share his interest in her and they would go from there.

There weren't that many people in the store at that time of night, but being cautious, she looked up again to check her surroundings and made eye contact with him. He held her stare, she smiled at him but then went back to looking for the exact brand of coconut milk she enjoyed.

She felt the closeness of someone to her. She looked to her right and locked eyes with him as he reached across her to grab some whole milk.

"I'm sorry for being so close to you, I really needed to get this gallon of milk." She could feel the heat of his breath on her face as he smiled at her.

His zesty smell captured her thoughts and made her lips curve into a sly smile. She gulped air and took a step back.

He secured the milk in his hand and stepped back from her smiling. He freed his right hand and extended it to her. "My name is Steve."

She looked down at his left hand trying to spot a ring on his finger closest to his pinky. Satisfied with not seeing one, she thought it was safe to flirt back with him. "My name is Pam."

"Pam." He let her name slowly roll off his tongue. He nodded his head staring at her. "I haven't seen you here before."

"So what, you work here or you come here every night?" She laughed.

He smiled. "No, I don't work here, but I do come here enough and I haven't seen you here before. What a pity." He winked at her.

She blushed. "Well, I normally do my shopping during the day at another store, but I had to get some things for my students tomorrow, and this was the only twenty-four hour store nearby."

"Oh, so you're a teacher. Brains and beauty. Nice."

"I see you're a smart man." She laughed.

He looked over his shoulder at her cart behind her. "Do you have everything you need?"

"Nope."

"Well, you wanna talk while we do the rest of our shopping together?"

"Okay." She positioned herself in front of her cart.

"Let me push that for you." He came up behind her and placed his hands on top of hers on the cart.

His breaths on her neck sent chills down her spine. She tensed up.

"My bad. I'm sorry for being so close to you. I was trying to show you how chivalrous I can be." He laughed.

She looked back at him and smiled as she moved out of the way to allow him to push the cart.

They walked slowly up and down each aisle of the entire grocery store savoring their time with one another. They stopped in the cereal aisle. Steve reached for five different boxes of the most sugary cereals and placed them in her cart.

"I see someone has a sweet tooth." Pam laughed.

Steve's eyes shifted. "Uh, yeah, I do. Let's get your candy and get out of here, it's late."

"I'm not in a rush, I was enjoying your company." Pam feigned pouting.

He moved closer to her. "Trust me, I'm enjoying your company, but I gotta get home and get some sleep for work tomorrow." He looked down at his watch. "Do you know it's after 1 am?" He faked a yawn.

"I didn't know it was that late. Okay, I guess we should get going." Pam stepped aside to let Steve regain control of the cart. They walked up to the registers.

She checked out at the register first.

She lingered near the Redbox machine while he paid for the items he accumulated walking through the store.

"You waited for me? Thanks." He smiled.

"No, with as long as you kept me in this store, you owe me a walk to my car." She laughed.

"Oh really? Well luckily for you, I was gonna insist that anyway."

He walked her to her car and helped her put her groceries on the back seat. "Look, Pam, I know we just met, but I would really like to get to know you more, so can I get your number and call you sometime?"

She smiled at him. "Of course."

Steve pulled his phone out and stored her number. She tried to get a look at his screen, but he kept it away from her. He called her phone at that moment, and she locked his number in her phone.

"Okay. Well, I guess I'll be talking to you soon." Her eyebrows raised as she lowered herself in her car.

"Definitely. Just text me to let me know when you get home."

"Okay. Bye."

He closed the door after she was completely in the car.

She smiled as she looked into her rearview mirror watching him wave at her. He still stood where her car was parked. Him waiting until she pulled off completely was yet another act of chivalry that night on his part. Surely she thought that meant he was a stand-up guy.

Pam came back to the present and turned over in her bed. She punched her pillow angry at herself that she met him that night.

She settled herself again in the bed and allowed herself to continue down memory lane with thoughts of him hoping it would somehow be therapeutic for her and end her mental torture. They seemed to be so honest and open with one another from the beginning. Every day during work hours they texted each other nonstop and talked during their lunch breaks rather than eating.

She remembered being so taken by him because in those first couple of days they talked about everything from the way they were raised to their hobbies. They even covered topics that most people would label taboo to discuss when first getting to know someone like their religious and political views.

When the first weekend arrived of them knowing one another, they had confirmed plans for a date at a restaurant outside of the city limits. She found that kind of strange, but she dismissed her query about it and agreed to meet him there. She was pleasantly surprised when she walked into the restaurant and took in the quaint and mellow atmosphere. His choice of the place made her like him even more.

She smiled in the present moment remembering how he ogled over her the entire night. She hadn't had a man's attention in a long time prior to meeting him, so she welcomed his attentiveness to her. She remembered admitting to herself that his talk of how much he liked her that night was so quick into their courtship, but she reasoned it was okay since she liked him as much as he seemed to like her in such a short amount of time.

After dinner, he walked her to her car. She normally didn't kiss on the first date, but he was so handsome to her that she accepted his invite that night to join in on a steamy kiss with him. They agreed to continue getting to know each other from that point on.

Everything seemed to flow with them, except for him being able to only talk to her during the work day or one specific hour during the evenings. But his limited times to talk didn't alarm her since she was so busy with work and school. She believed him when he told her he couldn't talk to her because he was either going straight to the gym after work or see about his mother and then rush to bed to get rest for the next work day.

Pam brought herself out of her memories and rushed to the bathroom to relieve herself of the three glasses of red wine she had consumed up to that point. She was glad that her memories of him were at bay for the moment as she sat in the bathroom. Thinking back of her time spent with him filled her with recollections she wanted to rid her memory of.

She made it back to her room and stretched out on the bed. The minute her head hit the pillow, more memories of her time with Steve flooded her thoughts. She sighed but allowed herself to continue down the path of remembering their time together hoping she would be all out of emotions and thoughts of them by the time she drifted off to sleep and could finally move on.

She tried not to, but she found herself smiling again thinking of how it was in the beginning with them, but there was a knock at her door that pulled her back to the present day.

"Who is it?"

Her father Melvin poked his head in the door. "Hey pumpkin. How you doing?" He opened the door wide.

"Wishing I could get a good night's sleep." Pam frowned.

"Want me to read you a bedtime story?" Melvin laughed leaning against the door.

Pam laughed. She loved how he was so attentive to her even at her age.

"Just making sure you're okay. I saw your car in the driveway, but it's awfully quiet in here. I want to make sure that you're okay?"

"Yeah, I'm okay dad."

"It's a Saturday night though pumpkin, why aren't you out enjoying yourself with friends or a special someone?"

She sighed loudly. "Dad, I'm pretty sure mom has told you that I'm not with him anymore, so it's not like I have somebody to go out with. I'm definitely not interested in starting something with someone new anytime soon."

"Yeah, she did, but I wasn't going to say anything about it until you came to me."

Pam frowned.

Melvin went over and sat at the edge of her bed.

"Look sweetie, I know you're grown and can do whatever it is that you want to, but I know how I raised you and I know that you're a good girl," Melvin laughed, "I mean a good woman, so I know you didn't set out to date a married man. But make sure moving forward you hear from God before you get involved with a guy. I would hate to have to go to jail at my age for someone breaking my baby's heart."

Pam smiled. "Thanks dad." She sat up and gave him a hug and playfully rubbed his balding head.

"Hey. Watch it."

They both laughed.

"Okay, so no man, but what about hanging out with your friends?" His eyebrows raised.

"School starts Monday, and I really want to relax today, not to mention Monica is married now with twins, Renee spends every waking moment of her day with her social work cases and clients, and you know Kim, probably out on a date somewhere."

"Yeah, you do have a lively and busy group of friends."

"Okay, well if you want some company you can find me in the living room watching a western."

"Thanks dad, but don't feel bad if I don't come down to hang out with you tonight."

"I won't sweetie." He leaned down smiling and kissed her forehead. He closed the door behind him as he left out.

Pam laid back in the bed smiling thinking about how she used to watch TV with her dad all the time when she was younger. He was a great man. She didn't understand how he and her mother had been together for so long because they almost seem like polar opposites. He was so laid back and smooth, while her mother was so demanding and blunt.

It must be true that opposites really do attract.

Coming back to the present, she laid there completely still for a minute. She hit the bed again wishing she could relax instead of being consumed with memories of Steve. *It's so pathetic that I'm in my early thirties alone on a Saturday night in my parents' house mulling over my past. How stupid of me to fall for that jerk. The signs were there, but I ignored them.*

With nothing else to do and not being sleepy, she allowed herself to relive more memories of her time spent with Steve.

She tried to make sense of why she gave in to him in the first place. According to her spiritual beliefs, she knew it wasn't right for her to be intimate with him before marriage, but her loneliness at the time and what she thought was being in love with him made her give in.

She thought it was the beginning of their forever.

She remembered back to a Thursday night that he called her around midnight.

"Hey babe. What are you doing?"

She remembered smiling, clearing her throat and adjusting her eyes to the darkness in her room before she spoke. "Well, since it is midnight and you know I have to work tomorrow I was asleep, but what's up?"

"I was wondering if I could stop by and see you. I have to make a run to the grocery store."

She loved the sound of his voice.

"You need to get stock in that grocery store. You always seem to be headed there whenever you call me." Pam laughed.

"What can I say, I'm a man. I gotta eat."

"But you only see me late at night before or after your grocery runs."

"I'm sorry babe. You know how I told you my schedule is at work. My mom still hasn't recovered from her surgeries. I had these responsibilities before I met you, but, because I wanna be with you, I'm trying my best to squeeze you in where I can. Shouldn't that count for something?"

She sighed. "Yeah, I understand that, I just wish things were different. I can't wait till you get that promotion you've been telling me about that will free up more of your time. And like I told you before," she cooed, "if you would introduce me to your mom, I could help out with her when you need me to."

He let out a loud breath of frustration. "Look babe. The promotion will happen soon enough, and as for my mom, now is not the time to meet her. But I promise you the moment her condition improves her house will be the first stop we make. And besides, you stay busy grading papers for your students and then your schoolwork for your degree. I wouldn't dream of asking you to help me out with her when you already have so much on your plate."

She smiled thinking he was so considerate of her schedule. "Well thanks babe."

"So, can I come over?"

She paused for a minute knowing what normally happened between couples that time of the night, but she felt her resolve was strong enough to keep his hormones at bay. "Okay."

She jumped up out her bed and rushed to her bathroom to make sure she didn't have crust in her eyes or slob dried up on her face. She brushed her teeth again in case they decided to have a make-out session.

She was rinsing her mouth out when her doorbell rang. She rushed to open the door.

"You got here quick." She laughed.

"I told you I had to make a run to the grocery store."

She closed the door behind him.

He stared at her with a ravenous look in his eyes she had never seen before. He wanted her.

"What?"

"You." He licked his lips.

Pam didn't have a bra on under her nightgown. It was cool in her house from the air conditioner. Her hardened nipples entertained him.

He continued to lick his lips as he scanned her body from head to toe.

She looked down embarrassed.

"Oh, I'm sorry." She crossed her hands at her chest to cover her breasts. She was embarrassed.

"Don't be ashamed. I love what I see." He smiled, zoomed his eyes in on her and moved closer to her.

He stood in front of her leering into her eyes.

Her closeness to him heightened her sensitivities. She knew she needed to be strong and only kiss him. She prayed that God would help her.

He placed his lips over hers and slowly kissed her as he groped her from her hips to her breasts.

He pushed her back against the door and pinned her hands against the wall.

He kissed her deeper and her arms closed around his neck pulling him in closer to her. She thought she would be able to control his hunger for her by simply holding him close to her.

His hand made its way between her thighs.

"No. We can't." She looked into his eyes hoping he remembered her rule.

"Come on, it's been like three or four months." His eyes pleaded with hers.

"I know how long we've been together, but I told you from the beginning how I felt about sex before marriage."

"But you're not a virgin."

That stung her. "So what. Just because I did it before doesn't mean that I have to continue doing it knowing it's not right." She pushed him back.

He smiled at her. "I'm sorry. I didn't mean for it to come out like that. I thought we were building something special." He pouted.

"We are." She interlaced her hands behind his neck and pulled him closer to her.

"So then if you really feel that way, sex should be a part of exploring our relationship." He pecked her on her lips as he squeezed her butt.

"Yeah, after marriage." She bucked her eyes at him.

"You are so sexy." He planted passionate kisses all over her face and neck.

She wilted in his arms.

She cleared her throat trying to gather her wits before she spoke again. "Steve, you've known this about me since we first got together." She playfully poked him in his chest.

He grabbed her arm and kissed her wrist and up her arm until his lips reached hers. His tongue explored her mouth again as he slipped his hand inside of her.

She jerked and pushed him away.

He feigned being shocked. He locked his hands on his head as he held it down for a second. He slowly lifted his head and rubbed his goatee. He let out a loud sigh. He clasped his hands together as if praying and shook them wildly. "You don't get it do you?"

"What?" She wasn't scared of him in that moment; she simply hated that he seemed mad at her.

He stepped closer to her with his hands behind his back. "I love you and I want to express myself to you in every way possible." He held her stare.

"Did you say you loved me?" She was genuinely shocked.

His face scrunched up. "You couldn't tell that by now?"

"I know the chemistry between us is strong, I just didn't know it was there yet."

He inched closer to her and placed his hands on the small of her back. "It doesn't take a long time for a man to know that he loves a woman."

"Okay, so if that's the case, then why aren't we talking marriage instead of sex?" She pursed her lips and crossed her arms at her chest putting all of her weight on one leg.

"Marriage is a big commitment." He took a step back from her and rubbed his head again.

"You act as if giving my body to you isn't." she bucked her eyes at him.

"I'm not saying that baby." He went back close to her and grabbed her hands to hold in his. "What I'm saying is that marriage is a commitment that has to really be thought out before people decide to enter it. It's not all that people make it up to be. It takes a lot of effort to make a marriage work."

"And it takes a lot of effort to get me. No ring, no nothing." She pressed her lips together.

He leaned his forehead on hers and his light brown eyes stared into hers.

Pam found them, him irresistible, but she knew if she did go all the way with him she knew it wouldn't be what God wanted. She looked back into his eyes as he spoke.

"How long do you expect me to wait?" He whispered to her as he kissed her on her neck.

"Until we get married, not a moment sooner."

He pulled back from her. "I need to go." He put his hand on the door knob.

"Hunh? Why are you leaving all of a sudden?"

"Because," he looked back at her, "I told you that I'm in love with you. I've tried my best to show that to you and you're still denying me, us, the chance to connect on that level. If I can't fully express myself to you, then maybe we shouldn't be together." He unlocked the door.

She grabbed his wrist.

She wanted Steve in her life. She reasoned, maybe if she had sex with him that night, it would put them closer to the altar. She wanted a future with him. Not wanting to give her approval out loud, as if verbally saying 'yes' to his desire would anger God even more than the sin she was about to commit, she nodded her head up and down.

He picked her up and she wrapped her legs around his waist. He had his way with her right at the front door.

Tears streaming from Pam's eyes brought her back into the present time. She wiped her face and shook her head thinking of how stupid she was giving into him to keep him around.

She hated remembering how good being with him felt to her body, but each time she slept with him it gnawed at her spirit.

After all that time down memory lane and downing an empty bottle of Merlot, Pam was still not sleepy. She sank deeper into her bed and helplessly went back to her memory of having sex with him for the first time.

They climaxed with her still pinned to the door.

He took him a moment to regain his full strength, but when he did, he kissed her on her lips and tried to push her gently aside to get out of the door.

"Where are you going?"

"I can't stay, and I have to go."

"What?" Her voice shrieked. "After that, you have to go? Why?" Pam asked confused and hurt.

He scratched his forehead as he looked down at his watch. "Uh, I just remembered that my sister was so distraught when I left her. Her boyfriend of ten years had just broke off their engagement. I need to get back to her."

Pam's eyebrows furrowed.

"Plus, I gotta get those groceries from the store."

Her nostrils flared.

"Plus, I gotta get some sleep tonight for work in the morning. I know that if I stay here with you, I won't be getting any sleep." He winked at her. He went in to kiss her on her lips, but she turned her head away from him.

"Don't be mad at me, babe, you know I would stay if I could."

Pam pushed him back from her. "Hold up, your sister? You've never told me about a sister, you've only mentioned your mother being sick and needing your constant attention." She frowned.

Wanting to be with him, especially after she had given herself to him, Pam accepted every excuse he gave her as to why he couldn't stay with her that night. She didn't argue with him anymore before he left.

Pam came back to the present and cringed thinking about how that night was the first of many that she allowed herself to be physically intimate with him. She always thought her resolve to not have sex with him would be stronger the next time.

How stupid was I to not see the signs that he was a married man? And why did I let us go on after I found out he was married? What kind of fool am I? I was never supposed to be the other woman. I was, I am better than that.

She hated the nightly cycle that had become her life, but it seemed like it would be another night of regret and tears as she dozed off to sleep.

Why couldn't he just be honest with me? She rolled over and the long dark brown layers of her hair draped her pillow as she let tears fall from her face. Her pillow was soaked with tears before she drifted off to sleep.

6

It was Monday morning. Pam had read over her list of students to make sure that she could correctly greet them each by name once they took their assigned seats.

The beginning of the day procedure called for Pam to stand in the hallway near the opened door of her classroom to greet students and monitor their noise level and behavior.

She smiled glad to see them calm and respectful as they traveled down the hall to their classrooms. She expected them to be rambunctious and a handful. Her day was off to a great start.

Pam walked in behind what seemed to be the last student to file into the room. She smiled as she watched them each search for their desks until they found one with their name on it.

Her attention gravitated to a very pretty dark-skinned girl refusing to make eye contact with anyone in the classroom. The girl didn't even notice Pam looking at her; her head hung low.

Pam scanned her seating chart trying to match the girl's name with her face. Pam smiled when she found the girls' name. *Sharday. Sharday.*

She couldn't wait to befriend the girl. She wanted to find out why Sharday seemed so sad and removed from the rest of the students; it was only the first day. It was supposed to be one full of hope and good promises for the kids, not gloomy as Sharday exhibited.

She stood up straight in front of her desk and cleared her throat.

The kids didn't know what to make of her. Silence fell in the room.

She smiled. "Good morning and welcome back to a new school year to each and every one of you. My name is Ms. Robinson, and although I'm new to this school, I'm certainly not new to teaching." She paused letting that settle in on the kids. "I was a sixth-grade homeroom teacher at my old school in Skokie."

One student interrupted her with a raised hand.

"Yes," she looked at his name tag, "James?"

"So why did you leave your old school?"

"Well James, I really wanted to come back into the city and teach kids like yourself."

Another inquisitive student raised his hand. She looked at his name tag, "yes, Michael?"

"What do you mean kids like us?"

"Well most of the kids at my old school didn't look like you and I-"

Another hand interrupted and spoke before being called on.

"What do you mean, they were white?"

She tried to contain her laughter of the students' bluntness. "Yes."

"Oh, so you wanna come back and help the po' folks." Michael said.

Another student jumped in the conversation before Pam could respond.

"Michael you can call yourself po' but I ain't. I gotta lot of stuff in my house. We got six TVs in my house." The girl smacked her lips and rolled her eyes at Michael.

Pam made a mental note to do a finance unit with the kids later on in the school year to talk to them about the poverty levels in America.

She was ready to get the discussion back on track. "No, I didn't say that. I didn't say anything negative. I'm black, you're black so why would I talk about you? That would be like talking bad about myself."

"True, true, true." Many of the kids said in unison nodding their heads.

Pam laughed inwardly at her class. She looked over at Michael, "to answer your question, I wanted to teach my own people and empower you all."

Pam continued to answer the kids' questions as they asked them. She smiled through the entire discussion believing that she was going to enjoy her school year because of the group of students she was blessed to have before her.

She continued the day with the ice breaker activities she had planned.

Even though Sharday was withdrawn during the

class activities, Pam found herself favoring the girl more and more as the day went on.

7

Pam stood in her classroom trying to think on happier times before Steve. She thought back to when her and the other ladies were extremely close, spending every chance they could together.

She never had much of a love life so she couldn't think back to one man or relationship that made her heart smile from memories of him.

She could only hope for brighter days ahead, but she wondered if God would ever forgive her for what she did and bless her with a love of her own, better yet, if she would ever forgive herself.

Pam knew that administrators did formal and informal observation throughout the year, but she was still unnerved by Vance's presence in her classroom. He had a clipboard so she knew he would be doing more than his standard walk through while he was there.

She walked around the room interacting with the kids, answering their questions, and engaging them as needed. In the midst of all of that, she looked up to see how intensely Vance was staring at her. His presence stirred something in her, but she didn't have the time or energy to worry herself with him. His attention to her wasn't enough to alarm the kids, but being a woman, she knew the look in his eyes meant more than mere admiration of her as a good teacher.

It was the day before they left for a middle school conference in Atlanta for four days and three nights. *If he's staring at me like this now with the students in the room, how will he be once we get to Atlanta? There won't be any kids or administrative duties there to keep him from talking to me as much as he likes.*

The conference would feature professional developments geared towards educating the participants on the latest strategies and schools of thought in relation to teaching middle-school-aged students.

Pam had looked at the agenda emailed to her and saw the daily sessions would end around 4pm. They scheduled dinners for 6pm nightly and the participants would be free after dinner or they could avoid dinner altogether. She decided she would take a novel with her to read to fill her time in the evenings, but she knew the staff tended to hang out with one another after the sessions ended daily. She was already thinking ahead as to what she would say to get out of being around him if it came to that point.

Yes, she thought he was a very attractive man, but she had no business even attempting to get involved with him. He was her boss and she still had demons from her past she had to deal with. She was in no emotional mood to be involved with another man.

Pam had to divide her attention that day between Vance's stares and Sharday's melancholy mood.

Something was even more alarming about Sharday that day. Although she didn't come off as the most confident young girl, her withdrawn demeanor was even more noticeable to Pam. She barely spoke even though she was always willing to talk during lessons and Pam tried to engage her in conversations and activities to integrate her with her classmates.

She couldn't stand to see Sharday being so sad. She made a mental note to speak with Sharday after school.

***

The school day had come to an end and Pam was eager to talk to Sharday.

All of the kids had left out of the room for the day except for Sharday. She took her time gathering her things to leave.

"Can you stay for a minute?"

"Yes ma'am." Sharday didn't look up at Pam.

Pam walked over to Sharday's desk as Sharday took her seat. "Is everything okay?"

"Yeah, I guess so." Sharday looked down as she played with the straps on her book bag on her desk

"Sharday, I hope you know by now that you can talk to me about anything, right?"

"Yeah," Sharday whispered.

"So is it something you want to tell me? What has you so gloomy lately?"

Sharday finally looked up at Pam. "I don't want to say something about it to you and then you say something to her, it'll make it even worse for me." She held her breath to hold in her frustration. Her eyes watered.

It was extremely quiet in the room.

Pam didn't want to push Sharday so hard that she wouldn't open up at all, so she remained quiet smiling at Sharday, waiting for her to speak.

Sharday looked up at Pam, saw the warmth in her eyes, and spoke again. "It's the kids in this classroom, especially Asia, she has them making fun of me. They make fun of how nappy my hair is and how dark my skin is. They talk about my clothes." Sharday pulled on her dingy button up and then used the sleeve of it to wipe her nose.

Pam heard the pain in Sharday's voice. Her heart went out to her. She made a mental note to speak to Asia the next time in class. In the meantime, she needed Sharday to perk up.

"Sharday, Sharday, will you look at me?"

Sharday slowly looked up at Pam

"Sharday, sweetie, you can't listen to what other people say about you. You are beautiful and never let anyone tell you otherwise." Pam smiled and winked at Sharday.

Sharday put her head back down. "But I don't feel like it."

Pam reached out to tilt Sharday's face back up

towards her. "Now you listen to me, you are beautiful. You are fearfully and wonderfully made in God's eyes. You are not ugly and you need to know that. God made you just the way you are supposed to be."

"I guess." Sharday shrugged.

"I know it's getting late, and I'm certain your mother is outside waiting for you. I'll let you go now, but remember that you are beautiful just the way you are."

Sharday stood up and grabbed her book bag and threw it on her back. "Bye, Ms. Robinson." She never looked back. She kept her head low as she walked out of the door.

Judging from the way Sharday left the room, Pam knew she had her work cut out for her with Sharday. She would've walked Sharday to her mother's car and talked to the both of them if she could, but she had to get home and get packed for the conference.

Her list of worries seemed to be piling up on her. Not only did she still have to deal with the demons of her past, but her mother was becoming more and more overbearing each day she stayed in her house. She now had the newly found burden to help Sharday discover her true beauty. As if that wasn't enough for her, she thought ahead to the next four days of the conference where she would have to be in close proximity to Vance. It would require her to deal with her ever-growing attraction to him and what seemed like his equal interest in her.

Out of all the things that seemed to be plaguing

her at that point, she was determined to get through to Sharday sooner than later.

8

Pam stood at the floor to ceiling window of the conference room and watched ducks wade in the pond one after the other. It looked as if they were creating a heart-shaped formation, but an eagle flew low over their heads and they broke apart.

Why does everything around me remind me of my broken heart and the shattered pieces of my past?

The host of the conference requested that everyone take their seats to start the session.

Pam pulled herself away from the pond scene and turned to find the table she would be sitting at. She spotted it easily when she saw Kim. They normally grouped staff from the same school together to confer about how key points presented during the session could benefit their school.

By the time Pam made it to the table, the only seat left was next to Vance. He smiled at her with his eyes as he pulled out her chair for her. She took a deep breath giving him a closed mouth smile. She knew it would be a long and interesting day.

Vance sat on one side of Pam and Kim sat on

the other side of her. She had no choice but to pass the notes written back and forth between the chatty duo.

Although she didn't let him in on it, Pam found Vance quite funny. He made a few jokes about how close the toupee´ on the speakers head was to falling off. And of course, Kim matched Vance's wit with her comebacks to his jokes.

Vance nudged Pam a few times trying to get her to join in on the laughter, but she declined him each time, so Vance continued passing his notes to Kim.

Pam grabbed a pen on the table and wrote a note of her own to Vance: *Mr. Sutherland, since you are the principal, aren't you supposed to set the professional example for us on how to behave at events like this?* She passed it to him. She crossed her arms at her chest and smirked looking straight ahead to the speaker.

Kim strained her neck to see what the note said and when she still couldn't see it, she motioned for Vance to hand it to her.

With hesitancy, he did so.

He must have agreed with Pam because he ceased his note-passing with Kim for the remainder of the session.

"You are such a fuddy-duddy," Kim whispered in Pam's ear.

Pam held her laughter in as she winked at Kim. She looked out the corner of her eye to see how Vance had sobered up his merriment.

His face was scrunched up. He was perplexed.

The three of them sat there silently for the

remainder of the session until the host announced that it was lunch time.

Pam didn't have much of an appetite lately. Guilt altered her desire to nourish herself. Instead of heading towards the line for food, she opted to go sit outside by the pond she spotted earlier that morning. She got up from the table and walked towards the exit but Kim stopped her in her tracks.

"And where are you going missy?"

She gave Kim a half smile. "Outside to sit by the pond."

"You're not going to eat with me? Eat this great spread they laid out for us?" Kim's eyes widened as she covered her chest with her hand pretending to be appalled by Pam's withdrawal.

"No, I just need some alone time."

Kim pushed the chair in that separated her from Pam and drew closer to her. She lowered her voice. "You okay sweetie? You're so dejected, not yourself."

Pam held her breath for a second, pondering if the burden of her recent past would be lifted if she shared exactly what she had done. No matter how close she was with Kim and no matter how supportive the sisterhood was when Renee and Monica revealed they each had abortions when they were in college, Pam didn't know how they would react to her indiscretion.

"Kim, I'm okay. It's just that ever since I moved in with my parents, I haven't had much alone time. You know I'm a daddy's girl, so I've been spending time with him watching TV or putting puzzles together. Then there's my mom, between her being so nosey and such a busy body, I've had no real alone time. I really need this lunch break to myself."

Kim glared at Pam a little longer. She was trying to gauge if Pam was holding something back from her. "You know I don't pry as much as the others and-"

"Say what now? You don't?" Pam laughed narrowing her eyes in on Kim.

Kim rolled her eyes, "No, I don't. Thank you very much."

They both laughed.

"Anyway, I can respect that you want some alone time, but if you're avoiding hanging with me or any of the other sisters because of what did or didn't happen with the guy you have yet to tell us about, you'll pay. Oh you're gonna pay big time sister." Kim stared at Pam.

"Whatever. I'm not hiding anything. I told you what I told you. Now leave me be." Pam laughed nervously as she walked away from Kim.

"I got my eye on you." Kim whispered smiling as she walked towards the buffet table.

***

Pam found herself a quaint spot near the pond, next to a gigantic tree trunk that had somehow formed into a bench-like surface. She sat on its smooth surface, wishing the anguish of her sin would smooth out in her spirit. She relished the shade of the tree and the heat of the sun mixing together to create a warm and calming temperature, unlike the cool fall weather that had begun to settle in Chicago.

She was lost in her thoughts when Vance came up behind her.

"Hey you."

The deepness of his voice startled her and sent chills down her spine at the same time. *My stomach, Are those butterflies?* She shook her head as she laughed out loud at herself.

She turned to face him. *Why are his eyelashes so long and show off his big bright eyes? Jeesh! Get it together before you speak to him.* "Hey." She gave him a half smile trying to mask any attraction she had to him.

"I wondered where you were after I got my food. I looked out of the window and saw you by yourself and figured you might want some company?" His voice went up a pitch hinting at his nervousness.

Pam looked up at him. "Um, I guess so."

He jumped over the tree trunk to sit next to her.

God! He smells so good right now. Pam turned her head in embarrassment as if he could somehow hear or read her thoughts. She laughed at the absurdity of it all.

He smiled as he looked at her. "Care to share what has you smiling over there?"

"Oh nothing, just a silly little thought I dismissed."

"Your secrets are safe with me." He laughed exposing his perfectly aligned white teeth.

She cleared her throat. "I promise it

wasn'thing."

"Okay. So why did you sneak away from the group? Was it because of me? Did I really rub you the wrong way passing notes?" Vance frowned.

Pam laughed. "No, I was only joking with you."

"Well you sure are a serious joker."

They both laughed.

Vance spoke up. "I came back to the table with my plate to eat with you and Ms. Williams, but she said you ran off somewhere. Is everything alright?"

"Yeah, I'm fine. It's that since I moved in with my parents--" She covered her mouth with her hand, hating that she let that part of her life slip out. It was none of his business, and she didn't want him to question her more as to why she moved in with her parents at her age.

"What?"

"I didn't mean to let it slip out that I am living with my parents right now." She looked away from him.

His eyebrows furrowed. "No need to be embarrassed. Things happen."

"Yes, they do." She said it slowly shaking her head. "And with that being the case, I haven't had much time to myself."

"Oh, so that's why you snuck away from us?"

"One of the reasons why." Pam mumbled under her breath as she turned her head away from him and twirled the ends of her hair.

Vance leaned in closer to her. "Hunh? What did you say?"

"Oh, nothing." She stared out across the pond

before finally looking up at him. "Okay, now that you know one of my secrets, you have to tell me one." She smiled at him.

"What?" He laughed.

"Yes, you have to tell me something about you that I don't know, that no one else at the school would know." She angled her body towards his.

He rubbed the neatly trimmed hairs of his goatee, contemplating exactly what to tell her. He didn't tell many what he was about to share with her, only his friends knew, but he was curious to see how she would react. "I'm a PK." He sat silently waiting for her response

"Mr. Sutherland-"

"Mr. Sutherland? Call me Vance, please." He lightened up for a second.

She loved the way he said his own name. The way it rolled off of his tongue with that deep voice of his. She cleared her throat and wiped her forehead of the sweat beads before she spoke again. "Okay, Vance, you're a PK- a preacher's kid- that's cool." She smiled at the new knowledge she gained of him.

He turned away from her and looked back out into the water.

She fully turned towards him. "Vance?"

He continued to look out into the water as if he hadn't heard her call his name.

"Vance? What's wrong with you being the son of a pastor?"

"I said I *was* the son of a pastor."

"Hunh? I don't understand, what do you mean?"

Vance scoured his thoughts for another topic

that might be of interest to her to change the subject; he came up with nothing. He looked down at his watch before speaking again. "Look at the time," he held up his wrist with his watch on it. "We should go back in now. The sessions will start up again soon."

"Yeah, I guess so." She slowly rose from the bench.

Vance held his arm out to assist her.

"Thank you." She smiled at him finally staring into his almost onyx-hued eyes and lost herself in them. He had to tug on her arm to get her to start walking.

He laughed. "You're glued to this spot aren't you?"

She laughed subtly. "No, we can go now." She wondered if he could feel her temperature rise as he continued to hold her arm.

They walked back to the meeting room in silence, enjoying each other's presence.

9

It had been months since all of the sisterhood had been around one another. Pam pretty much avoided them and Monica was so busy with her twins and planning all of the fabulous events she did as an event planner, the four of them hadn't been in the same room since the last time they attempted to pry Pam's recent life past her shut lips.

Kim, Renee, and Monica had all resolved that they would make Pam open up that night.

They decided to play catch up at Monica's house. They figured they could be entertained off and on by the twins while they were there.

Pam stood at the door and took a deep breath before she rang the doorbell. She hoped the ladies would lay off of trying to pry into her life. She was glad to be out of her parents' house for the night. She wanted to enjoy the company of the sisterhood.

She finally rang the doorbell.

"I got it." Kim's loud voice could be heard from the other side of the door. She opened it and smiled. "Hey girl."

"Hey you." Pam smiled.

"Girl hurry up and get in here. It's chilly out there." Kim pulled Pam into the house and slammed the door.

They embraced one another.

"I should've known you'd already be here." Pam smiled.

"You know it. I try to spend as much time with my niece and nephew as I can when I'm not working or with one of my male friends." Kim winked.

Pam rolled her eyes.

"Whatever. And being around them reminds me of why I don't want to have kids."

Pam gasped feigning being shocked.

"Whatever. You know I love my independence. Having kids would cramp my style."

"It's crazy how you're a teacher but you don't want kids." Pam said.

"Uh duh. Being a teacher is a major reason why I don't want kids. Raise them at school and at home? No thanks."

Pam shook her head. "You are too much. You say that now, but when that 'one' for you comes along, you'll be singing a different song."

"Okay, act like you have amnesia and don't know me if you want to." Kim said. "I don't care who comes along, they ain't changing my mind. This here tiger won't be getting any new stripes." She extended her hands at Pam in a clawing like motion causing Pam to laugh hysterically.

Pam caught her breath. "You are a mess."

"This I know. And no more than you, keeping

secrets from us and all. Mmmhh hmmmm. Come on girl." Kim grabbed Pam's coat and locked her free arm with Pam's and pulled her into the den.

Pam slowly shook her head. *Lord please let this be the only mention of me tonight and what I haven't told them.* "In Jesus' name, amen," She mumbled the last part.

Kim looked over to her. "Hunh, what did you say?"

"Nothing. Just clearing my throat."

They walked into the den arm in arm.

Pam smiled seeing Monica plant kisses all over Keith junior's face while Renee played in Kalia's thick curly hair.

"Say hey, Auntie Pam," Monica said to Keith Jr.

He smiled as he waved his hand slowly from side to side and batted his long eyelashes at her.

"Hi, handsome " Pam leaned in towards him to tickle his chubby little stomach, and he fell back laughing hysterically and drooling.

"What took you so long to get here?" Monica pouted.

"My nagging mom, traffic, life, who knows. Hey, get off my back."

They all laughed.

Pam inched over to Kalia playing peak-a-boo as she neared her. Every time Pam peaked from behind her hands, Kalia almost jumped out of Renee's hands in ecstatic joy.

Keith appeared from the kitchen. "Hey Pam. I haven't seen you in a while." He walked to her and embraced her in a hug.

"See, we're not the only ones that think you've been keeping yourself from us." Kim stuck her tongue out playfully at Pam.

"I've missed you." Keith hugged Pam even tighter. "My mom misses you too."

Pam's heart sank thinking about how long she had been away from Keith, Renee, and Kim's mom, Mrs. Williams. She helped to balance out Pam's teenage years when Pam's mom seemed to be too overbearing.

Pam's phone alerted her to check her notifications on Facebook, but she didn't bother to do so. She knew the messages were from Steve. He didn't have a Facebook account before they met, but he created a page once they made them official. It was cool to her at first that he didn't have many friends on his page. She liked her men out of the spotlight; but in light of everything that happened between them, she realized that he created the page to keep tabs on her. He never added any of his friends because then his truth would have been exposed. She shook her head realizing he never even put up any photos of himself on there.

"Pam. Pam." Monica yelled.

"Hunh?" Pam wondered how long she had been in her trance.

"Say goodbye to the twins. Keith is taking them upstairs so that we can get to our girl time." Monica said.

"Bye you adorable little muffins." She rushed to kiss their cheeks as Keith held them. She made a promise to herself that she would visit them more often. She wanted them to know who she was the way they recognized Kim and Renee.

The twins stared over Keith's shoulder laughing at their mother as she played peek-a-boo with them until they could no longer see her.

"Okay, ladies, let's get down to business," Monica said.

Pam's eyebrows furrowed. She wasn't sure, but she sensed she was the "business" to get down to.

Kim bucked her eyes at Pam. "Yes, she said business. We have business to tend to now."

Monica shook her head at both Pam and Kim.

"Don't look confused like that Pam," Monica laughed. "We told you the last time we were all together that it wouldn't be the last of us interrogating you until we found out exactly what's been going on with you."

"Yeah girl, I'm the first to tell y'all to mind your business when y'all trying to figure out who I'm seeing at the current moment." Kim sat there smacking loudly on grapes as she looked over at Pam.

"We never have to ask because you willingly tell us." Monica laughed.

Kim looked up at the ceiling aimlessly. "Yeah, you're right."

They all laughed.

"But like I was saying, I would consider myself the voice of reason when it comes to us not digging too much into each other's personal lives-"

Monica bucked her head at Kim.

"What?" Kim shrugged her shoulders.

"Don't what me. You're over there acting sanctimonious like you don't delve into our business when it was you who threatened me with grocery store trips and workouts at the beginning of my weight loss journey."

Kim stopped reaching for grapes to put in her mouth, squared her shoulders facing Monica, and narrowed her eyes in on her. "So you're telling me that you didn't appreciate my tough love?"

Monica sunk back into her oversized chair. "No, I didn't say that." She pouted.

They all laughed.

Monica jumped up out of her seat. "Okay, okay, okay. I love your tough love Kim." She blew her a kiss. "If it weren't for y'all's support I wouldn't have all of this." She slowly spun in a seductive circle framing her small waist and ample, yet toned hips and butt. "I bounced right back after the twins." She snapped her fingers and flipped her hair over her shoulder.

They all fell out in laughter.

"You are a nut Mon, but what I think Kim is trying to say to, Pam, is that we've always been so close. No matter what has happened in our lives whether good or bad, we've always been willing to share it with one another. If not everyone in this circle, at least one other person knew what was going on in each of our lives." Renee ended her sentence crossing her legs Indian style on the floor.

"Yada, yada, yada. Yeah, I was saying what she said. It's so mind boggling to us how you managed to have and lose a man that none of us met, move out of the house you love, and buy a condo in the city all under our noses. We weren't privy to any of the details of what was going on with you." Kim popped more grapes into her mouth.

"Yeah Pam, I mean we could've helped you pack and move. Went house searching with you for the new place. And of course, we would've liked to meet and drill the man that you were in love with." The corners of Monica's mouth turned down.

Pam paused before she spoke. She took a deep breath before trying to plaster a smile on her face. "Ladies, sisters, for one, I wasn't in love with him, I-"

"Let me stop you right there. If you're going to lie to us, then I'd rather you not speak." Kim cocked her head at Pam.

Pam sat silent wondering how she even thought she could possibly lie to her friends. They had known each other since middle school and they knew each other very well. They could easily detect each other's varying moods and emotions. She knew it was a stretch trying to keep the ladies from questioning her about him and admitting that she loved him. She wasn't sure how much she would reveal to them.

She took a deep breath and sat up more in her chair. "Okay ladies, yes I *was* in love this past year."

Renee jumped up and clapped her hands. "Yes, you're in love. Another wedding soon." Renee sang.

Kim looked dumbfounded at Renee. "Renee calm down, she said *was,* you know past tense, meaning not anymore, el finito, sayonara sucka.

There will be no wedding starring her as the bride anytime soon."

Monica worked hard to contain her laughter as she saw the joy vanish from Renee's demeanor. She shook her head laughing at how Kim could be so *real* sometimes.

Pam found herself laughing at Renee's slumped shoulders. "Okay, I guess I was in love. I didn't introduce you all to him because we didn't have time. We were selfish with the little alone time we could squeeze into our schedules."

"Mmh. He must've been a busy man." Renee said.

"You have no idea." Pam mumbled.

"You're right. That's the problem. We have no idea. Fill us in." Kim said.

"He was busy and so was I." Pam rolled her eyes at Kim.

Kim shook her head.

"You had the kind of man in your life that kept your attention the way he did and you didn't allow us to really celebrate that with you." Monica jumped in.

"Trust me you guys, you all *don't* want to know why we didn't work out. Shoot. I wish that I could erase it from my memory. My life." Tears seeped from Pam's eyes.

Kim and Renee rushed to crowd Pam's feet.

Monica went over and sat on the arm of Pam's chair and rubbed her shoulders.

The comfort of her friends sent her emotions in overdrive and she wept for quite some time before she mustered up enough strength to speak to them again. "Thanks, ladies." She wiped her eyes.

Monica squeezed her tighter and she dropped down into the oversized arm chair with Pam.

"Trust me you all, I want to share all that happened between he and I, but it's not something that I'm ready to open up about yet."

Renee bucked her head. She looked hurt. "But we've always been so honest and open with one another." *Yeah right, maybe I shouldn't keep pushing her to open up, because if they only knew what I did...*

"Yeah, like you told me about your abortion in college." Kim turned her head away from Renee.

Renee's eyes shifted for a moment trying to figure out how to turn the attention away from her. She certainly wasn't ready to deal with that topic again. She wrapped her arms around Kim's neck lovingly and smiled as she spoke. "Aw sissy." She kissed Kim's cheek. "How long are you gonna stay mad at me about that? I told you I was sorry. I'll never ever ever ever keep another secret from you," she looked at the others, "or from any of you all again." She hugged Kim tighter. "Now will you forgive me already, please?" Renee wasn't superstitious, but she crossed her fingers behind Kim's neck with what she had said to the ladies.

"Oh shut up girl, I forgive you. Now let me go so that I can breathe."

They all laughed.

"The spotlight is on Pam now." Kim redirected the group.

Pam shook her head.

"Ok, since you insist on not telling us about him yet, is there anything else in your life that's weighing you down that you're willing to share with us? Please, something?" Monica laid her head on Pam's shoulder.

"Ok, well there's this girl in my class, Sharday, whom I adore. She's so beautiful, but I can see that she doesn't know that yet. I think God laid her on my heart to minister to her." Pam wondered would God really use her to minister to Sharday even though she herself was a mess.

Monica perked up at the mention of Pam being a blessing to a young girl. "So what do you plan to do to help her?"

"By being a listening ear and confirming her beauty everyday with little gestures and possibly even some class lessons on differences in people and the need to embrace them."

"Okay, sounds like a plan." Monica said.

"Yeah, I hope it works. There's another girl in the class I know I'll have to get through to as well. And then there's my Principal."

Kim unglued herself from Renee to focus on what Pam had to say about their boss. "Mr. Sutherland? What about Mr. Sutherland?" Kim smirked having witnessed the weird chemistry between Pam and Vance at the conference in Atlanta. She could tell they had a connection. Pam skipped lunch with her every day during the conference but she could look out the window over to the pond to see Vance sitting with Pam. They both seemed at ease talking to one another. She remembered how he hung out with them for dinner each night instead of venturing off with the gym teacher. During the sessions, Vance was full of questions where Pam was concerned. She noticed the exchanges of glances between them and the in-depth conversations they had during break times. She knew that Pam would come clean to her soon enough about her interest in Vance, but she wanted Pam to fess up about the mystery guy in that moment.

"Whatever, Kim." Pam rolled her eyes. "I don't know what's up between us. It's not like he flat out told me that he likes me, but I see the way he looks at me. How it feels when he's around." Pam let her words trail off, she lowered her head and caressed the throw pillow she cradled remembering back to the many engaging conversations and alone time they spent together during the conference. She knew he took advantage of every free moment of their time at the conference to be around her. She smiled.

"Well, why is that such a bad thing?" Monica asked.

"I have no business getting involved with a man right now. I don't think God will bless me with love after what I've done." Tears streamed down Pam's face as she lowered it into the pillow.

"Listen here," Kim stood up, snatched the pillow from Pam's face and wagged her finger in Pam's face. "If you're gonna keep being so secretive with whatever happened between you and the guy you won't tell us about, then don't sit here weeping over him and what happened between y'all but not share it. Damn you! Would you tell us already." Kim threw her hands up in the air and sashayed back over to the couch before she fell back on it huffing and puffing.

"Kim, don't be so insensitive. Clearly it's something too painful for Pam to even share with her closest, dearest friends, whom she should know wouldn't judge her but instead support her and help her cope with whatever happened." Renee poked her lips out in sadness.

Monica worked hard not to laugh during the seriousness of the moment. Kim had all but had a temper tantrum with Pam and Renee had just laid one of her most guilt-ridden speeches yet on Pam.

"Besides Pam, God is a loving God. He doesn't dish out His wrath on us the way He could for our behavior at times. Remember, He said He would remember your sins no more. He cast them out into the sea the minute you asked for forgiveness. You asked for forgiveness, right?" Renee asked.

"A thousand and one times," Pam mumbled.

"Well then, He's forgiven you sweetie. Maybe it's time you forgive yourself," Monica said softly, leaning her head onto Pam's shoulder.

Kim was now off the couch. "Forgive me for not wanting to be around you all anymore right now."

"What?" Renee's eyebrows furrowed as she stared at Kim.

Kim looked directly at Pam. "You, my friend, are full of it, and I would rather be around the twins right now than to be around someone who doesn't trust me enough to share what's bothering her the way it's clearly been eating you alive these past months."

"Kim, don't be like that towards Pam. She'll open up to us soon enough." Monica looked at Kim.

"Monica, you can shut up too." Kim stormed out of the den and headed upstairs to the twins' room.

Renee shook her head as she looked up at Pam and Monica. "Now you all know that my momma didn't raise us like that."

They sat silent for a minute staring at one another before they all broke out in laughter.

"Okay, now that Kim's foolishness has passed, I reminded you that God loves you and doesn't even remember your sin. You said you asked for forgiveness, so tell us the 411." Renee said.

Pam narrowed her eyes in on Renee. "Really?"

"What?"

"Ladies, I love you all, but I need some time alone now. I'm gonna head home, well, to my parents' house."

"No Pam, don't go. Okay, we'll stop pressuring you to tell us. Just stay. There are so many other things we can talk about." Monica said.

"Thanks Mon, but I really am tired and I wanna lie down. See you all again soon though." Pam walked to the front door and stepped into her boots as she wrapped her scarf around her neck.

Monica came and stood behind her and helped her put her coat on. She hugged Pam tightly. "I pray that you would soon let go of this heavy burden that you're carrying. I love you."

"I love you too."

"Yeah, I love you too," Renee called out from the den.

Monica stood in her doorway and watched Pam as she closed the door to her car in the driveway.

Pam sat in her car letting it warm up before she pulled off. She sighed and watched her breath fog the windows.

Her phone notified her that she had new Facebook messages. She knew it was Steve, seeing as though it was his only way to communicate with her, he had been messaging her nonstop.

She clicked on her Facebook app, went to the settings option and deactivated her account. Making it his last mode of communication with her. She wanted nothing ever to do with him again.

10

Vance being the principal of Jensen Academy.

He enjoyed working with teachers to create the best atmosphere to enhance the education of the students that walked through the doors each day. Fortunately for him, this school year brought an additional joy with entering classes daily. Pam was now a part of his staff. He seized every opportunity he could to speak with her, and when talking to her wasn't always possible, he would sometimes stand at her door peering through its large picture window admiring her.

He loved how passionate she was about teaching her students and inspiring them to be all they could be. He admired her sense of style; she was all woman, and her clothes always hugged her curves perfectly.

One particular Friday afternoon, he sat in her class listening to her engage the kids on how to write a good narrative when his mind drifted back some months to a staff appreciation dinner he hosted.

He remembered the moment as if it had happened yesterday. The dinner began at 6pm that evening. Vance had been mingling with the staff for the first hour of the night. He looked around frequently noticing that Pam and Kim hadn't made their arrival yet, but he knew they would be coming since they RSVP'd for their dinner choices.

He was sitting at a table directly across from the door, conversing with the gym teacher when she walked in and slipped into the coat closet to stow her black knee length pea coat. Under it she had on a black form-fitting cocktail dress. She wore black three-inch stilettos that laced around her ankles accentuating her toned legs. She smoothed out her dress as Kim beckoned her to exit the coatroom.

Clutching her minute black handbag, she entered the cozy sized ballroom at the hotel. She stopped to pose for a picture being taken by a professional photographer hired by the school clerk to capture still shots of the night. As she stood their grinning with an enchanting smile waiting for the flash to signal that the photographer had taken the picture, Vance sat in awe of her.

It wasn't that he hadn't taken notice of her beauty before that moment; rather everything, from the lighting, to the music, to the small crowd, was in its rightful place, to reveal what was hidden in his heart for her.

Although she looked stunning in that little black dress, that showcased curves of her unknown to him, it was her eyes that spoke to him. He never recalled seeing her with makeup on, and even though she only had eye shadow and mascara on that evening, the two seemed to magnify the beauty of her eyes and the soul of her within.

Pam settled deeper into his heart that night after she exposed a hidden talent of hers, singing. She wowed her co-workers with her sultry voice as she therapeutically sang a Jill Scott song. He remembered that throughout singing the tune she avoided looking at him as she sang in her tantalizing voice. He thought that was cute.

Vance's flashback was interrupted by the school's public announcement system, "Mr. Sutherland, you are needed in the cafeteria."

Vance left Pam's classroom wishing he would have had more time listen to her voice or take in her beauty for as long as he wanted to, but being the principal of Jensen wouldn't allow that.

He would have to discuss his problem with the "Gents" later on that night.

11

Pam paced her classroom floor trying to keep calm as she spoke to the receptionist from the moving company on the other end of the phone tell her how there would only be one mover there to help her that day. If she wanted more movers, she would have to wait until next weekend.

"So you're telling me that there's only going to be one man helping me move all of my heavy furniture from my storage unit to my third floor condo?" Pam realized her classroom door was open, she lowered her voice.

"I'm sorry Ms. Robinson for the mix up, but we only have one mover available this evening."

"And what about tomorrow? Sunday?"

"Again, only one mover this evening. All of the others will be dispatched to other jobs."

"When I made my appointment with you all a month ago, I let you all know how much furniture I had and what floor it would be taken to. You all assured me you would be able to handle the job in a timely fashion. How can one man do all of that? I'm not a weak woman, but I certainly can't help him with the heavy furniture I have."

Vance tapped lightly on her open door.

She turned towards him embarrassed that he may have heard her yelling at the receptionist. She smoothed down her shoulder length hair under Vance's stare and lifted one finger signaling him to give her a second. She turned her back towards Vance to reconvene her phone conversation.

"I'm sorry Ms. Robinson, but we only have the one mover available for you. Do you still want him to come?"

Pam took a deep breath before she spoke. "Yes. Send him to the address I gave you all with the truck, I guess he and I will figure it out."

"Sorry Ms. Robinson. Enjoy the rest of your day." The receptionist said in an apologetic tone.

"Yeah. You too." Pam ended the call.

She knew she wouldn't last one more week in that house with her mother, and besides, her condo was ready.

She turned to face Vance.

"I'm sorry for interrupting your call. I was up here making sure there were no more kids left in the building when I heard your voice. You sounded distressed and I came in to make sure you're okay. Sorry for being so intrusive." Vance's big eyes softened as he stared at her.

Pam averted eye contact with him. "It's okay. I appreciate you coming to check on me, thanks." She rounded her desk and sat down in her plush rolling chair trying to give her knees relief from the continual walking she had been doing during the day and especially during her phone call with the receptionist.

"Pam, I mean Ms. Robinson-"

She smirked. "It's okay, you can call me Pam."

"Okay, Pam, again, I didn't mean to eavesdrop or be in your business now, but since I know what's ailing you, I would love to help."

With her eyes wide, she looked up at him. "Mr. Sutherland-"

"Remember, I asked you to call me Vance." He smiled and winked at her.

She blushed. She held her head down for a second to gather her composure in his presence. "Vance, I couldn't ask you to help me move all of my stuff."

"You didn't." he laughed.

She smiled. "You're right, I didn't, but it's a Friday night, we've had a long week and I'm certain you have other things, people that can occupy your time tonight."

He laughed. "Are you fishing to see if I have a girlfriend?" He walked closer to her.

Pam jumped up out of her chair. Shock laced her face. "No, please don't think that I'm being unprofessional with you or implying anything improper, I was just saying-"

Vance laughed. "Pam, it's okay. Relax, please. I didn't say that you were being unprofessional. We're two co-workers talking after work hours. We can let our hair down now. Well, maybe just you, seeing as though mine doesn't hang." He rubbed his hands over the deep waves in his low haircut.

They both laughed.

"Okay, so what do ya say to me helping you?"

"I guess, if you don't mind. I really can use your help. Thanks again." She smiled.

"Cool." He clapped his hands together. The loud echo of his clap reminded him to calm down. Too much of his excitement to see her again was showing.

Pam giggled.

"Okay, so where and what time should I meet you?"

She played with her phone as she talked to him with her head low preventing eye contact with him. "Give me your number and I'll text you the address to the storage place, the time to meet me there, and my new address as well."

He slowly pulled her phone from her hand and stored his number in her contacts list. He then gently placed her phone back in her hand, smiling and noting that not once had she looked up at him in the past few minutes.

"I'll text you soon," she smirked as she looked up at him.

"Cool. See ya later." He smiled and oddly high-fived the wall as he walked out whistling.

***

"Thank you sir." Pam handed the mover a one hundred dollar tip as he stood in her doorway.

"No problem. Thank you."

He walked out of her condo and she closed the door behind him.

Pam fell back against the door and breathed a loud and long sigh of relief. *Finally, I'm in my own place.*

There was a loud crash in the living room.

"What the-"

"Sorry, I didn't mean to drop it," Vance called out from the living room.

Pam palmed her forehead in amazement "I thought I was finally alone, I forgot that he was still here." She mumbled. She took a deep breath and walked down the long corridor of newly waxed chestnut hardwood floors that lead to her open kitchen and common area at the back of her condo.

She searched her thoughts trying to come up with a nice way to tell Vance that she would prefer to be alone for the rest of the night.

She stopped short of the opening to the space to see him squatting over the broken pieces of the floor vase he had broken. Although it was her favorite piece she had picked up at a vintage shop years ago, what used to be the beauty of it paled in comparison to Vance's well defined back that her eyes locked in on. Her eyes danced with every muscle that redefined itself in his back as he moved about picking up the broken pieces of the vase.

No. I can't be attracted to my boss. So what he's fine, smart, charming- Stop it! Stop looking at him like that Pam. You have no time to concern yourself with a man.

Pam laughed at herself for the internal conversation she was having.

Vance stood up with the broom in one hand and the dust pan in the other. He turned around and looked at her. "You okay?"

She smirked. "Yeah, I'm okay. So, I'm certain that you're ready to go. Thank you so much for your help." She walked over to her granite countertop to grab money from her purse. "I guess I'll see you Monday at work." She held two hundred and fifty dollars in her hand extending it to Vance as he came towards her from the disposing of the broken vase.

His eyebrows furrowed as his eyes narrowed in on her. "What's this for?"

"For your help."

"No need to pay me, I would do anything for you, anytime." Vance lowered his head shaking it. He didn't mean to say that out loud. He stuffed his hands into his pockets.

Pam tightened her lips. She tried to hide the mixture of merriment and confusion that settled in her stomach. She folded her arms at her chest.

There was weighted silence between them.

Vance slowly lifted his head and locked eyes with Pam.

She lost herself in his big bright eyes before she cleared her throat to speak. "I'm sorry if I offended you by offering you money for helping me, I didn't want you to think that I took your time and help for granted."

"I would never think that." He shifted his weight from one leg to the other as he kept his hands stuffed in his pockets.

The warmth in his smooth deep voice, his muscular stature towering over her, and his proximity to her was unsettling to her. She knew she had to get him out of her house as soon as possible. "You won't accept my money, maybe I can bring you lunch one day or all next week to show my gratitude for your help?"

He laughed. "Pam, you don't have to repay me at all. It was my pleasure helping you move in." He looked around the room full of boxes. "In fact, I want to finish helping you, because unless you get some help from someone and soon, you'll be unpacking for months to come." He smiled.

She looked around at the boxes in the kitchen and living space knowing they didn't compare to the boxes she had to unpack in the other rooms of the house. She knew she needed and would love his help, but with her uncertain and growing attraction to him and most certainly the stain of what Steve had put her through, she didn't think that it was wise for her to be around him alone often and for long.

She sighed. "Yeah, I know it will be a big task for me to complete, but if I do as much as I can everyday, I'm certain it will get done sooner than later." She laughed and turned around tripping over a box at her feet. Her body didn't touch the floor, because in one swift motion, Vance jumped out and grabbed her from behind around her waist and kept her from falling. She dangled in his arms with her feet high off the ground as he held her petite frame tightly.

"Pam, let me help you." He allowed his face to bury itself in her hair taking in its sweet berry fragrance.

Pam took a deep breath and relaxed her body in his arms.

He slowly let her down to the floor and held on to her waist until he knew for sure that she had her balance.

She wiped her face trying to compose it before she turned to face him. When she did, she looked into his deep onyx-colored eyes. "Thank you for coming to my rescue again."

"For you, anything." He lightly bit into his tongue regretting letting that slip out.

She backed up some from him. "Look, I appreciate everything you've done for me tonight and the continued help you want to give to me, but I don't want to be a burden on you any longer. Besides, it's a Friday night, you should be out partying and enjoying life."

"I could say the same for you."

"Touché." Pam laughed.

"Seriously Vance, go and enjoy your night. I'll be fine here. I'll turn on some music and get to unpacking. It's the weekend. I have some time. I'll be fine."

Vance ignored her. He walked over to a box labeled stereo equipment and tore it open. He didn't worry himself with trying to mount anything on any walls yet, he only wanted to get the music going so she would feel more comfortable and start unpacking.

There were no CDs in sight for him to play, instead, he plugged in her surround sound speakers and attached them to his phone. He felt he had the right playlist to energize them while they unpacked.

Pam's eyebrows raised as she stared at him all the while he moved around her living room as if he were in his own home. "What are you doing?" She asked when she saw him plug his phone into her speakers.

"Giving us some music to listen to while we work." He never turned towards her while he spoke. He wasn't going to let her put him out. He planned to stay and help her that night as long as she stayed awake.

Us? Pam laughed to herself as she moved the box she almost fell over against the wall. She tore open a box labeled "kitchen". She started placing its contents in the cabinets above the countertop.

"Well at least let me get you something to eat. How about pizza?"

He smiled at her as he rubbed his stomach. "Cool, I am hungry."

She laughed. "Well luckily there's a pizza place right around the corner and they guarantee speedy service. How do you like your pizza?"

"However you like yours." He pushed aside some boxes clearing a path.

She turned from him blushing. She googled the pizza places number and placed the order.

Smooth R&B filled the room as Vance came and stood next to her in the kitchen. She had filled one shelf, but she struggled on her tip toes to place dishes on the shelf above it.

"Here let me help you before I have to put my cape on and rescue you again." He laughed and grabbed the dishes from her.

"Oh whatever Mr. Sutherland." She playfully hit him on his arm but she quickly regretted doing so because after all, he was her boss.

His eyes widened.

She laughed knowing why he looked at her the way he did. She was still being too formal with him. "I'm sorry, Vance. I'm sorry for hitting you. I didn't mean to, I was only joking." Pam's palms were sweaty.

He looked at her. *Man, she is beautiful, even standing here panicking, nervous and all.* He laughed. "Pam, it's okay. I know that you were joking. Would you relax already? Do I need to pick another song, playlist to help you calm down?" He headed towards his phone.

"No." She grabbed his arm to stop him. "I love this song. Let it play." She slowly took her hand from his arm and pushed back the hair from her face that refused to stay in the ponytail on top of her head.

"Okay. So you like the singer, Eric Roberson?"

"Yeah, I do."

"Cool, he's pretty much the rest of that playlist."

They continued opening up boxes and Pam instructed Vance exactly where she wanted things to go.

He enjoyed being in her presence, so he gladly did as he was told.

"Shoot!" Pam gripped her hand as blood dripped from it.

"What?" Vance turned around to see Pam's bloody hand. He leaped over boxes to get to her. "Come here." He cupped her hand in his as he led her over to the sink and turned on the cold water.

They let the water run over her hand for a while before the water in the sink finally drained clear.

He looked up from the sink into her eyes, "do you want to go to the ER to get this checked out?" Concern laced his voice.

Pam worked hard to keep her face from showing the overwhelming warmth she felt from his sincere concern for her. She wanted to enjoy the moment with him, but if she had been so deceived by Steve, she couldn't trust herself with another man anytime soon.

She smiled before speaking to him. "I'm okay. See." She held up her hand for him to see that the gash in her palm wasn't as deep as he thought it was.

"I see. Ouch." Vance winced. "Exactly what happened?"

"I reached into the box to take out my cutlery rack. I thought I was being careful grabbing it, but I guess a knife had fallen out of the holster and I grabbed it palm first. It cut me before I realized what happened."

He pulled on her, "come on, I would feel better if a doctor checked you out. You know, make sure it's not infected or something."

She deadened her body weight so that he couldn't pull her from the spot she was standing in.

"What?" He looked at her.

"Vance, I promise I'm okay. Thank God-"

Vance shook his head laughing.

Pam was taken aback by the tone in his laugh. "It's not as bad as it seems. I'll be fine. I'll get some ointment, gauze, tape, and wrap my hand up. God always looks out for me, no matter how foolish I tend to be." Pam walked towards the bathroom.

"You really think that?"

She stopped and turned back towards him.

His hip leaned against the island as he folded his arms across his chest.

"Hunh? Think what?"

"That there's some mystical deity watching over the earth? Guiding our footsteps? As you seem to think."

Pam's forehead slowly creased as she stepped towards him. "Yes, I do believe that there is a God. I know for a fact that God exists."

He laughed and his eyebrows raised as he spoke. "Oh really? What evidence do you have to prove that?"

"For one, I just *know*. That's what the Holy Spirit does, it reassures me that God exists. Then there's nature. The human mind couldn't shape the waters and the land the way God did. There's other stuff too." She folded her arms at her chest and cocked her head staring at him.

He laughed again. "Like what?"

She snarled at him before speaking. "There's so much other stuff seen and unseen that attests to God being God, but you have to be a believer to understand it. To understand His love. His ways."

He braced his hands on the island countertop and stared at them before he looked back up laughing to speak to her. "So you think this God that you speak of loves us?"

"Yes, I do." Her eyes bulged at him.

"Ha!" He rounded the island and came closer to her. "Love? A loving God wouldn't allow death, disease, homelessness, and the other calamities to go on in this earth the way they do if he *loved* us the way you think He does."

Pam took a deep breath before speaking. He was now adding too much to her emotional and mental plate. It was already so full with the servings of her past. "Mr. Sutherland, God gave man dominion over the earth, who then forfeited it to Satan, but because God is so gracious and loving, He sent His son Jesus to the earth to redeem man through His birth, death, and resurrection. We, mankind, have authority over what happens in the earth. Is God all powerful? Don't speak, I'll answer it. Yes He is. Can He use His might to do away with all of the suffering of the world? Again, no need to answer that, I will. Yes, He is more than capable of doing that, however because He honors His word, He won't take back the authority He gave us. We can't blame God for what we allow and sometimes cause to happen, so yes, I do believe that God is loving and cares so much about us that when we go through situations He's there to comfort us, like when…" Pam caught herself from almost sharing with Vance what had been weighing so heavily on her heart and conscious.

He saw so much anguish in her eyes that he wanted to reach out and wrap his arms around her, but he remembered that he needed to get his point across to her. "If that's your definition of a loving God then I can do without that God. That God that would allow people who say they love him to be killed senselessly." Vance stepped back from her with his hands entwined together above his head. He turned his back to her and walked away with his head down. He needed to regain his composure in front of her.

Pam noted the tormented tone in Vance's voice. For all the strength she had seen in him before. His spirit seemed so weak at the mention of senseless killings. She wondered what the story was behind his disbelief in God.

Her eyes shifted in confusion before she finally decided to speak. "Look Mr. Sutherland, It's been a long night. Thanks for your help, but honestly I would prefer to be alone now." Pam allowed her shoulder to rest against the wall as she folded her arms at her chest. She winced from the pain in her hand. She remembered she never made it to the bathroom to get the supplies to tend to it.

Vance stared out of the double sliding doors that led to her balcony on the back of the building. He laughed as he turned to her. "Why am I Mr. Sutherland again to you?" He stuffed his hands in his pockets with his shoulders high.

She completely fell against the wall. She refused to look at him. "I think we got too comfortable with one another tonight. I say we go back to being boss and employee." She dropped her head.

"But tonight was like picking up where we left off at the conference in Atlanta. We got to know quite a bit about one another."

"Evidently not the important stuff." Pam mumbled adjusting her stance on the wall.

"Hunh?" Vance said.

"Nothing." Pam shook her head.

"I thought you enjoyed our convos, my company? I definitely enjoyed yours."

"Yeah, that was at the conference. We haven't talked outside of work since then."

"No fault of my own." Vance mumbled as he rubbed his temples.

Pam smirked. "What did you say?"

"Oh nothing." Vance gave her a half smile.

"Clearly, the more we talk, the more personal we get with one another. It's too much for me right now."

"Wow." He walked towards her. "Look, I'm sorry, for asserting myself tonight with my beliefs and questioning yours. Let's forget the conversation ever happened. Let's get your hand fixed up and get back to getting you unpacked." He now towered over her leaning against the same wall she leaned on in the corridor.

Without saying anything, she lifted herself from the wall and from under him. She walked over to the speakers and disconnected his phone. She grabbed his coat from a chair at the kitchen island and walked back over to him with the coat and phone extended to him at arm's length. "No, I think it's best if we call it a night."

He opened his mouth but closed it. He did it again, but his tongue remained encased at the bottom of his mouth. His arm reached out to grab her as she walked ahead of him down what seemed like the longest corridor he had ever traveled but to him it seemed as if his arm wasn't long enough to reach her. He made it to the door as she stood there with it opened. She had the whole third floor of the building to herself, so luckily for him he wouldn't have to worry about some neighbor witnessing her putting him out.

He stood as close to her as he possibly could as he put his coat on hoping his proximity to her would comfort her enough to let him stay a little longer.

She opened the door wider signaling for him to exit through it. "Thanks for sacrificing your Friday night for me. Enjoy the rest of your weekend."

He obliged her and walked out into the carpeted hallway.

"Goodnight." She sighed.

He fixed his mouth to say one last thing to her, but she quickly closed the door in his face.

Vance knew he needed to unload on the guys as soon as possible.

12

"What am I supposed to do fellas?" Vance sounded to his friends as they took their seats in the Gibson's Steakhouse, their favorite restaurant in downtown Chicago.

"About what?"

"What now?"

Anthony and Marcus, respectively launched their questions at Vance hoping that he wasn't going to begin ranting about how hard it was to find a woman who thought like him or at least willing to accept his beliefs.

Vance paced himself as he began to speak knowing that the guys had grown tired of him continuing to believe differently from them even though they all had grown up in the same Christian church. Vance smiled and raised his hands in protest as he spoke, "let me say all that I have to say before you all start lecturing me."

The rest of the guys nudged each other while laughing. They knew it would be one of his "me" discussions.

"Seriously though, I have never mentioned Pam to you all before because I didn't know what to make of her and I."

"Pam." Darius stated as if he were a nine-year-old boy teasing another boy about a crush on a girl.

"I knew it had to be about a woman." Anthony stated matter-of-factly.

"So what's her story or problem? As you say they all have." Marcus said dryly.

Again the men hurled their questions and comments at Vance so fast that he had to choose which one to address first. Vance planned to ignore Marcus' statement since he and Marcus had thick tension between the two of them when it came to his beliefs.

"Pam is a teacher at my school. She is smart, sexy, charismatic, beautiful, wise, funny, gorgeous, can sing, and she dresses well," Vance ended his statement with a wide grin covering his face.

"Think you used enough adjectives to describe her?" Darius said sarcastically.

"Did I mention she was beautiful?" Vance replied cunningly.

"Yes." They all concerted.

Marcus huffed. "Dare I ask what her problem is?"

"She's saved." Vance said despondently.

Attempting to be funny, Darius asked, "saved from what?"

"Saved from sin because of what she thinks Jesus did for her," Vance said sarcastically.

Marcus stood from his seat and threw three twenty dollar bills on the table. "I'm out." His voice and tone were deafening.

All of the men, including Vance, knew why Marcus had left but no one dared to bring up the subject. To lighten the mood, Darius began to share a tale of the last time he tried his hand at his stand-up comedy act.

13

It was the first Monday morning after Christmas break. Most people would see a two-week vacation as a relaxing experience, but not when you are a teacher. They often spend most of their time catching up on things they can't comfortably do during the school year, like possibly hanging out with friends, traveling, holiday festivities, and of course sleep; the greatest commodity of them all for a teacher. But then there's the looming desire to grade papers and do lesson plans with the hopes of either catching up on late work or working on future items on their to do list, in hopes of being ahead when school resumes.

Pam would have relished in any of these activities during her break, but they all seemed impossible with the weight of her guilty conscious and heavy heart derailing her focus.

She thought to cut off any and all ties and modes of communication with Steve, but since she closed all of her social media accounts, he emailed her several times over the break telling her how much he missed her and how his life hadn't been the same since she was no longer apart of it. He stressed how he wanted her back.

Thoughts of him and her kept her up all night. She hoped her restlessness through the night didn't show up on her face that morning.

She was looking at herself in the mirror inside of her coat wardrobe trying to will the dark circles under her eyes away when she heard a knock at her classroom door. She closed the door to the closet slightly to see that it was Vance. She opened it again to shield herself from him. *What is he doing up here? I can't take another heated religion convo with him right now. And I don't get why my heart races so whenever he is near me.*

She smoothed out her hair, applied more gloss to her lips, and then smoothed out her dress before she closed the closet door.

She slowly walked over to her classroom door to open it for him. "Good morning Mr. Sutherland. You know, this is your school. You can open any door in it you want to."

"Mr. Sutherland?" He gave her a half-smirk. "Okay. I see you really are back to being formal with me. I know I could've used my key to come in, but I never want to infringe on your privacy like that, that's why I knocked, I respect you. And because I do, I came up here to apologize to you again."

She folded her arms across her chest. She went back and forth from looking down at her shoes to barely making eye contact with him as she spoke. "Look Va- I mean Mr. Sutherland-"

"I like it when you call me Vance." He said in a low, soothing tone as he leaned against the wall.

She stepped back from him. "Mr. Sutherland, I appreciate all the text and voicemail messages you sent expressing your apology. I know I didn't respond to any of them, but I read them and honestly I do accept your apology. As I said before, I would prefer," she refused to look up at him, "I think it's best if we keep our dealings with one another strictly professional. If it's anything work related, you can reach me via my work email or speak with me while at work, otherwise…"

"Otherwise what, don't talk to you at all?" He grinned as he stood up flat-footed towering over her as he came closer to her.

His cologne invaded her senses and she had to force her feet to move her body backward away from him otherwise she was afraid she might reach up and kiss him. He seemed to have that affect on her, which she finally admitted to herself.

There was so much more he wanted to say, share with her, but with how tense she seemed at the moment and the fact that the bell rang signaling that the kids would be coming up the stairs any minute, he figured it would be best to let his feelings for her lie dormant for now.

***

"Welcome back my lovelies. I'm so glad to see each of you all back today. Hopefully, you're well rested and ready to finish the rest of the school year strong."

Many of the students laughed.

Her eyebrows furrowed. She scanned the room. "What's so funny?" She smiled.

Michael said. "Kids don't sleep on breaks. We stay up all night snapchatting and chilling." He led the class in laughing, all except Sharday.

"Okay, so if you didn't rest, what did you do?" She rested her bottom against her desk and folded her arms across her chest readying herself to hear their many Christmas break stories.

The hands flew up.

She called on and listened to each student as best as she could but her attention continued to stray to Sharday. Sharday seemed so detached from the glee that was going on around her.

Pam had the kids to journal and share their post-Christmas joy with a partner in their groups until the end of the period while she took attendance, did the lunch count, and collected homework packets, among a few other morning tasks she needed to complete.

The bell rang alerting the class that it was time for them to go to gym. It took them a minute to all get completely quiet because a few of them felt it was absolutely necessary to finish sharing with their partner what they did over the break.

Pam stood at the door with her arms folded at her chest with a stern look on her face. Silence covered the room. All the students sat up straight in their seats making sure their areas were neat and free of clutter.

Pam called table numbers until all of the students were lined up. She opened the door as she reminded them of the expected hallway behavior and then allowed the girls to exit first, the boys followed suit.

The gym room was next door to Pam's classroom, so her and her student's didn't have far to travel. She stood in the silent hallway with them waiting for the gym teacher to come out and get her students.

"Hello room 305. Come on in." Mr. Bonner spoke to the kids in his normal cheerful voice.

Each of the students high-fived him as they walked past him.

Pam smiled at him and pointed at Sharday at the end of the line signaling to Mr. Bonner that she would keep Sharday. Pam grabbed Sharday's arm before she could enter the gym room.

Sharday kept her head down the entire time never questioning Pam's retention of her.

"Come with me for a second." Pam smiled at Sharday.

"Okay."

Pam and Sharday entered the classroom and Pam closed the door behind them. "Have a seat." Pam signaled for Sharday to sit in the comfy chair next to her desk she allowed students to sit in when she held one on one conferences with them to help them with anything they were struggling with in class.

"Sharday, look up at me sweetie."

Sharday slowly lifted her head to Pam with tears puddling in her bottom eyelids.

"Sharday, I hope you know that you can talk to me about anything, right?" Pam handed Sharday Kleenex as the tears rolled down Sharday's face.

Sharday began to pant as she spoke. "Ms. Robinson, I'm just so tired of them all. Especially her. I hate her." Sharday screamed and buried her head in her lap.

Pam rubbed Sharday's back for comfort before Sharday sat back up. She stared at Sharday as Sharday wiped her face trying to regain her composure and even her breathing.

"Sharday, are they still bothering you? I talked to Asia about it. She said she wasn't bullying you, but she knew of some kids in the class that were."

Pam's heart sank.

"She's lying. She's the main one and she's gotten worser since you had the talk with her. I told you it wouldn't help. They mess with me even more, that's why I haven't said anything else to you about it. I mean some of the kids stopped bothering me after your last talk about cyber bullying, but her and a few other ones didn't. They keep putting up fake memes of me on Facebook, Snapchat, Instagram, all of the sites I'm on. I tried blocking them from my page, but they always find a way to get messages to me and I could see what they post of me on other people's pages. Why doesn't anyone like me? Why am I not pretty like her? Why did God make me this way? Black and ugly."

Pam's eyes welled up with tears. She had enough. "Sharday, stand up now. Right this minute. Listen to me. You hear me?"

"Yes ma'am."

"You are not ugly. Your black is beautiful." Pam pulled Sharday over to her coat closet and pulled the door open so that Sharday could stare at herself in the floor-length mirror attached to its door. Pam stood behind her.

"Look at you. Just look at you." She carefully cupped Sharday's chin until her face was parallel with the mirror. "Your black is beautiful. No one else in the world has these exact almond shaped dark brown eyes." Pam pulled at the corners of Sharday's mouth pulling it into a smile.

Sharday giggled a little as she sniffled.

"No one else has these gorgeously aligned teeth like you do. Smile so *you* can see them."

Sharday forced the corners of her mouth upward into a smile. She tilted her head to get a closer look at her teeth.

"I tell you what, I bet if you smiled more several things would happen."

"Like what?"

"I'm certain you would feel happier. Others would get a chance to see that gorgeous smile of yours and it would make them happier."

"I don't believe that." Sharday allowed the corners of her mouth to droop again.

"Stand up straight and smile again." Pam barked out the orders.

Sharday stood up straight, but she still frowned.

"Why won't you believe me?" Pam looked into Sharday's eyes in the reflection in the mirror.

"Because even if what you said is true about my eyes being beautiful or smile being gorgeous, that still doesn't change how dark my skin is or how short and nappy my hair is." A tear seeped from Sharday's eye.

Pam grabbed Sharday's shoulders forcing her to face her.

"Sharday, you and I are almost the same color. I love my color."

"We aren't the same color Ms. Robinson." Sharday held her forearm up to Pam's arm exposing that she was indeed a shade darker than Pam.

"So what we're not the same color, you're still beautiful."

"No I'm not. I'm black and all scratched up from being such a tomboy when I was in the fourth grade. Your skin is all smooth and pretty. It looks so soft."

Pam shook her head. She was ready to continue to affirm Sharday's beauty, but Sharday cut her off.

"And you can't compare me to you, because not only am I darker with scratched up skin, but my hair is short and nappy while yours is long and straight. Why did God make me ugly like this?" Sharday leaned into Pam and wrapped her arms around her waist as tight as she could while she cried as hard as she could.

Pam rubbed her back thinking something had to be done to stop Asia's ongoing bullying and to get Sharday to see how beautiful she was.

Sharday's cries subsided.

Pam pulled Sharday away from her. "Sharday, do you want to go to gym now or stay in here until the end of the period?"

"Please Ms. Robinson can I stay in here with you? Please? I don't want them to see me crying. I'm tired of them seeing me cry."

"It's okay sweetie. You can stay in here. I have to leave to make a phone call. I know you love to read a lot, why don't you grab a book and read."

Sharday walked over to her desk and grabbed her novel that she was almost done with after checking it out days earlier. She settled herself on a beanbag in the classroom library.

Pam said a prayer to herself for this storm to pass in Sharday's life and how she could play a part in helping Sharday to see how beautiful she is.

With so little time left in the period, Pam scurried downstairs to the teachers' lounge to use the phone in there.

She passed by Vance in the hallway reprimanding a group of boys for disrupting the learning environment in their classroom with a paper ball fight. While he should have been chastising the boys, his eyes locked with hers and they held his thoughts and tongue captive until she pried her attention away from him and continued to head down the stairs to the teachers' lounge.

The boys giggled at him. "Mr. S., why you looking like that?"

"Mind your business. Like I was saying…"

Pam was grateful that there was no line for the phone. She still might have a chance at making her call and going to the bathroom before she had to race back upstairs to get her class from gym.

She picked up the receiver and dialed the number next to Asia's name on her class list. "Hello, may I speak with Mrs. Brown?"

"How you doing Ms. Robinson? Remember I told you I'm no longer a Mrs. the divorce isn't finalized yet, but I consider myself single. What has Asia done now?"

Pam shook her head at how nonchalant Asia's mom was in questioning her daughter's behavior.

"I'm sorry to bother you but-"

"No worries, just sitting here with my soon to be ex-husband pestering me."

Pam could hear him cooing in the woman's ear. She refocused her thoughts to the task at hand. "As we spoke about it before, Asia has not stopped bullying the student I told you about. The girl says that it was worse while they were away during the break."

"Ms. Robinson, I did what I thought was best to stop Asia's disrespectful behavior the moment you first called me about it, but as you say, it hasn't stopped. I don't know what more to do, so I'mma send her daddy up there. Maybe him being up there with you all will show her that her behavior isn't right."

"Thank you. Is it possible for him to come up here after school today?"

"Hold on…"

Pam could hear Asia's mom talking to the man in an irritated voice while he sounded determined to get her in bed.

"Okay, he said he'll be up there when school gets out."

"Thank you so much."

"I hope this gets settled once and for all." Asia's mom said.

"Me too. I look forward to meeting her father after school. Take care."

"Okay. You too... Get away from me..." Asia's mom said as she ended the call.

Pam laughed inwardly at how men mess up a good thing and then go crawling back to it begging for forgiveness. If Asia's dad was as bad as the mom made him out to be, she hoped the mom stuck to her guns and left him alone. *As women, we don't have to settle for any old fool that tries to run game on us. We're worth so much more.* She knew she needed to repeat that often to herself.

Pam rushed to the bathroom and then to get her kids from gym.

The day continued on with Pam noting how Asia did little things throughout the day whether it be in class or even at lunch trying to intimidate Sharday.

Pam was grateful when the bell rang at the end of the day. She could dismiss her class and get to the meeting that would hopefully make things better for Sharday.

"Asia and Sharday, you're going with me."

Asia scrunched her face up and squinted at Sharday as she dragged her book bag on the ground behind Pam.

***

Pam sat in the conference room at a round table with Sharday and her mom to the right of her and Asia awaiting her dad to the left of her.

Pam prayed inwardly that the meeting would indeed end Asia's bullying of Sharday.

Pam was completely engrossed in a conversation with Sharday's mom when she noticed two distinctive scents enter the room.

Having been around one earlier that morning she knew Vance had entered the room and she hated how the knowledge of him being in there did something scintillating to her body. But the other scent, it was one she laid under many a night. She had dismissed its owner months ago. She prayed whoever was wearing that distinctive cologne wouldn't turn out to be the one from her dreaded past.

"Ms. Robinson," Vance called out to her.

The way he called her name held a certain longing.

She slowly looked up at Vance and immediately noticed the man next to him.

It was Steve, Asia's dad, the man she unknowingly had an adulterous affair with for a little over a year.

14

Her stomach churned and she worked hard to keep her face and body language from showing the contempt she held for him.

He smiled seeing her and the upward curved line on his face stretched wider as he walked closer to the table to shake her hand.

"Ms. Robinson." He stood next to her waiting for her to shake his outstretched arm.

She mustered up all the professionalism she could to oblige his request but snatched it back feeling his fingers caress the back of her hand.

"Nice to meet you." He smiled at Pam again and took the empty seat next to Asia.

Asia turned towards him. "Daddy." She jumped out her seat to hug him wrapping her arms around his neck.

He stared at Pam staring away from him the entire time Asia embraced him.

Vance took a seat in the corner noticing how intently Steve stared at Pam in contrast to Pam seeming so uneasy in Steve's presence.

Sharday sat in amazement thinking she had never witnessed that Asia before. The one she encountered daily seemed to have horns instead of ponytails.

"Asia have a seat. I'm not here for a good reason." He finally pulled his eyes away from Pam to look at his daughter.

She immediately sat down and straight up in her seat with her hands folded in front of her.

"Mr. Brown." Pam shuddered at the memories of screaming out his name when they had sex. For over a year she hoped that she would soon share his last name, little did she know there was already a woman and three kids wearing that badge of honor, or perhaps shame.

She cleared her throat pushing the bile back down. "Mr. Brown," she barely looked at him, "I asked you to come here today because despite the lessons I've taught on bullying and the several phone conversations I've had with your wife about Asia's behavior, Asia has continued to bully Sharday."

He pulled his attention away from Pam to stare at Asia. "Look at me."

Asia quickly looked up at him with such a childlike innocence. "What do you tell me when I ask you are you still messing with the girl?"

She said nothing.

"Do you hear me talking to you?" His voice dropped a register.

"Yes sir." Her response was barely audible through her shaky voice.

"Well answer me then."

"I tell you that I'm not doing that anymore."

"Yes, that and that you two in fact are good friends now."

Sharday's mouth dropped wide open and she hit the table.

Sharday's mother gave her a stare that let Sharday know she had better calm down.

Sharday crossed her arms at her chest letting her chin touch them.

"Mr. Brown, I witness the sadness Sharday experiences on a daily basis because of how Asia is still treating her. I've taught units on bullying and self-love trying to the get the bullies to stop and the ones being bullied to love themselves in spite of. I've spoken to your wife…" Pam stared at him with seething anger in her eyes.

Steve cleared his throat and shifted in his seat. "About this matter. She's shared with me where she thinks Asia's behavior change stemmed from. She said she's tried what she could to stop Asia, but she thinks you seem to be the only one to make Asia straighten up." She compressed her lips together tightly trying to prevent any bitterness she had towards Steve spew from her mouth.

"So you've been lying to me?' Steve turned Asia's chair towards him so that he could get a better look at her.

"No daddy."

"Apparently you have. I take up for you when your mother tells me about this all the time saying you would never lie to me, but I see you have been."

"No daddy, no. I'm sorry." Big droplets of tears ran down Asia's face as she tried to jump up and sit in her daddy's lap.

"No. Stay in your seat and wipe your face now."

Asia was losing the race of keeping her face clean as the tears continued to flow.

Steve turned and looked at Pam and then pulled his eyes away from her to look at Sharday's mom. "Ma'am, I'm sorry, I didn't raise Asia to be mean and evil as you all say she has been."

He then looked at Sharday. "I'm sorry for the way my daughter has been treating you. You ARE a beautiful young lady and you deserve respect from all of your classmates, especially my child."

He looked back at Pam. "May I ask what her mom said the reason was for her acting this way?" His stare bore holes into Pam.

Vance remained in the corner tense about Pam's body language during the meeting.

"Sir, I think that's something you'll have to talk to your wife about."

"Ex-wife." He corrected her.

"Whoever she may be to you, you need to talk to her about it." Pam sniped.

Steve smirked. He looked back at Asia. "You and I are going to have a long talk this evening young lady."

"I'm sorry daddy." Her tears continued to flow.

"That won't cut it this time. Now apologize to Sharday. And you better dig deep inside yourself and mean it, because if I so hear that you even look at her in the wrong way again, you have yet to experience what I will do to you. Do you hear me?"

"Yes sir."

"I don't care what is going on at home you are no better than the next child here and you have no right to take your anger out on anyone."

The sternness and bass in his voice made Asia jump in her seat.

"Now apologize and mean it."

Asia wiped her face then looked over to Sharday. "I'm sorry for bullying you and being mean to you."

Sharday stared at her for a moment checking her sincerity. "Why should I accept your apology? Ms. Robinson has made you do it before, but you kept on messing with me."

"I'm sorry Sharday. I promise I am." Asia's eyes pleaded with Sharday.

"Okay, but I promise you Asia, if you mess with me again, I'mma knock you out."

Everyone's eyes bulged staring at Sharday.

"Sharday, control yourself. You will do no such thing." Sharday's mom said.

"I promise I can't take it anymore, so I'm giving everybody, especially Asia a fair warning."

"Sharday, I swear I quit. I don't like seeing my daddy so disappointed in me." Asia jumped out of her seat and grabbed his neck.

He embraced her. "I love you sweet pea, but you can't treat people any kind of way. You're still in trouble, but we'll talk about it later."

Pam stood up. "Well, I guess this is finally settled."

She looked to Sharday for confirmation.

Sharday gave her a half smile.

Pam turned towards Sharday's mom and shook her hand. "Thank you, Ms. Fletcher for coming up here."

"And thank you, sir." Pam barely looked at Steve.

Vance stood up. "Come on Ms. Fletcher and Mr. Brown, I'll walk you all out with the girls."

"Thank you sir." Ms. Fletcher said as she grabbed her purse from the back of the chair.

"Mr. Sutherland, if you don't mind, I need to speak to Ms. Robinson for a second." Steve said.

Pam shuddered.

Vance wanted to go stand by her side but knew he needed to remain professional.

"Asia, go and wait by my car, I'll be out in front in a second."

Vance hesitantly walked the girls and Ms. Fletcher out leaving Steve alone in the room with Pam.

"Pam, you look great." He turned to see if anyone else was around. "I see you have your hair down and straight. That's what I first noticed about you, your long beautiful hair. I've missed you baby." He walked towards her.

She jumped back. "Stay away from me." She lowered her voice hoping not to cause a scene that would send her coworkers in the room to investigate the commotion.

"But Pam, you know I love you."

"I thought I made myself clear to you the last time we spoke." She was now pointing at him with the veins in her neck noticeably throbbing. "You never loved me. You we're married. And I don't date married men. Haven't I made it clear by not responding to you all of this time that I want nothing to do with you. You disgust me."

"But Pam, we were still together after you found out I was married, and I know that's because you loved me then, and you still love me now. Only love would make you be so upset with me right now."

He tried to walk closer to her, but she grabbed a large stapler off of a nearby desk signaling to him that she would use it as a weapon if need be.

"Pam, think about all that we shared. It's not too late for us to work things out."

"Steve, please leave now."

"Pam."

Kim was walking past the room when she heard the deep affectionate voice of a man call out her friend's name. She peeked her head inside the room.

Vance had made it back up the stairs and was heading back to the conference room.

"I said leave now." Pam screamed unconcerned with who would hear her.

Vance heard the alarm in her voice from the hallway and ran past Kim in the doorway to inside of the room. He saw the hardened look on Pam's face and noted her vice-like grip on the stapler she was holding.

Kim had now come to Pam's side.

"Mr. Brown, I don't know what's going on but I clearly heard P- I mean Ms. Robinson asked you to leave. Sir, you need to do so now." Vance stepped in front of Steve.

Steve laughed quietly. "Okay Mr. Sutherland, I'll go." He looked past Vance to Pam. "Talk to you soon Pam, I mean Ms. Robinson."

Vance had a few inches of height on Steve, so he gladly towered over him. "Is that a threat?" His nostrils flared.

"Calm down, Mr. Sutherland. She's my daughter's teacher. I will see her again. Y'all take care now." He put his hat on his head and tipped it as he walked out the door with Vance on his heels.

"Sweetie are you okay?" Kim pried the stapler out of Pam's hand.

"No, I think I'm gonna be sick." Pam cupped her mouth with one hand and gripped her stomach with the other as she rushed from the conference room headed to the bathroom.

Vance came back as Kim was about to chase after Pam. He stopped Kim in her tracks. Panic riddled his face and voice. "What was that all about?"

"I don't know. Excuse my language boss man, but I'm sure as hell gonna find out."

15

Pam had cried herself into a splitting migraine. Her vision was blurry as she raced home after work.

She had no intention of ever seeing Steve again after she broke it off with him. She was desperately trying to start her life anew. Seeing him that day and him still trying to get with her was too much for her.

She shook her head in disgust at herself knowing that she had slept with and been in love with a married man.

Steve is Asia's father. It was one thing when I found out that he had a wife and I didn't break it off with him immediately because of his promises to leave her, but to know his daughter, to see how our affair hurt her and turned her life upside down, I'm so sorry God.

The moment she got her door open she fell to her knees weeping.

"I'm sorry God. I'm so sorry God. I know I shouldn't have given my body to him God and we weren't married." Her voice trembled. "I know the moment I found out he was married I should've left him alone God. I'm sorry." Her head was pounding and she couldn't see through her tears. "I was in a lonely place at that time God, I felt like you had forsaken me not giving me a love of my own. I tried to do things my way…"

She didn't even wait to hear from God; Pam let her words trail off figuring He wasn't listening to her anyway. She picked herself up off of the floor and entered the half bath near the front door. She looked at herself in the mirror and despised how she had let the weight of her sin take a toll on her health and heart. She was experiencing the worst migraine she had to date since she learned of Steve being married.

"I don't know how to get past this." She screamed and dropped her head and hands to lean on the sink.

There was a knock at the door.

Pam dismissed the knocking and continued to mop over the sink.

Whoever was at her front door began to beat on it until it shook.

What disrespectful idiot is at my door unannounced and beating on it like that.

She hoped ignoring whoever was at the door would send them away, and soon.

The pounding on the door continued. "Pamela Shanice Robinson, you open this door right now before I tear it off of its hinges. And I know you're in there, I saw your car out front." The pounding continued at the door.

"Kim, go away," Pam screamed out as loud as she could amid her intense migraine.

"I will not. You better open this door little girl before I tear it down."

Despite her mood, Pam smirked a little thinking of how since Kim was the oldest of the ladies by a few months and that she sometimes called each of them "little girl" when trying to get them to see things her way.

"Come on Pam, please open the door for us." Monica said loud enough to be heard by Pam, but hoping her volume was low enough not to disturb Pam's neighbors in the building.

"She better before I make a scene." Kim barked.

"Come on Pam. We're all here for you. Whatever it is you might as well tell us. We've already kind of figured it out anyway." Renee blurted out.

Kim popped Renee in the arm and then leaned in to whisper to Renee and Monica. "Why'd you say that? If this breakdown is because of the student's father I told you about, then he may be the guy she's never told us about. You may just have closed the door on us for good even though it literally is closed."

Renee's eyes shifted from Monica to Kim. She was bewildered.

"Don't worry about trying to understand Kim now, let's focus on getting in there." Monica pointed at the door to Pam's condo.

Pam stood in the doorway of her bathroom. She didn't want to share the details of her affair with Steve with the ladies, but she knew the rest of the sisterhood would only continue to meddle until they knew *all* of what was going on with her and devise a way to help her.

She went back into the bathroom ignoring the pounding on the door and splashed her face with cold water.

The frigid water was like electricity to her charging up every possible nerve ending and strengthening her migraine. She jumped and grabbed her temples trying to dull, if not end the pain in her head.

She exited the bathroom and walked to her front door. With one hand on the knob and the other pushing against the door, she let her head rest on the door. *Should I really let these nosey girl's in here right now?* Surprisingly to her, she chuckled a little bit knowing that she better let them in.

She stepped back unlocking and opening the door all in one motion.

Renee's eyes bucked seeing the ghastly sight that was Pam.

Monica poked her lips out in sadness for the torment she saw etched on Pam's face.

Kim shook her head walking towards Pam. "Look at you." Kim's fingers got tangled in the mess that was Pam's hair. "You're better than this. Get in here so we can fix you up and find out what's going on with you." Kim walked past Pam as if she knew where she was going in the uncharted territory that was Pam's new home. She stopped in the bathroom and grabbed some items to beautify Pam. "Take her in there somewhere and find seats for us, some water, snacks, but do something productive with yourselves." Kim ordered them all.

Monica and Renee sandwiched Pam with their arms around her rubbing as they walked down her long foreign hallway of rooms. They reasoned the wide open space at the end of the hallway had to be the common area of the condo.

They walked into it to see a beautiful earth tone rich open concept kitchen with glass cabinet doors and complimentary varying textures between the floors and the countertops. The décor mirrored Pam's classy yet down to earth persona.

Monica and Renee were both sad that this moment with Pam in such disarray was the first time they had ever been into their best friend's beautiful new home. They used to do everything together, so it was hurtful to each of them that Pam had made such life-changing decisions in the past year without them.

Renee cleared items off of the loveseat while Monica propped Pam's fragile body up on hers until Renee cleared the path for her.

"Well I'll be damned." Kim shouted as she entered the common area. She stopped near the entryway and scanned the space from left to right. She slowly allowed her eyes to travel the twelve feet high walls until they reached the vaulted ceiling.

She looked over to the ceiling above the kitchen area to see a beautiful circular sky roof perfectly centered over the island in the kitchen. She walked over to it and rubbed her fingertips over the cold earth tone granite countertop.

"Kim, what are you doing? We're here to see about Pam."

"Monica, I'm taking this all in right now."

"Taking in what?" Renee asked.

"Our best friend's new place. We might not ever see it again after today." Kim walked over to where the rest of the sisterhood was seated. Since the other two encased Pam, Kim pulled up an ottoman and sat right in front of the ladies. She didn't want to miss a thing.

Kim handed Pam the towel she was holding.

Pam put it up to her face. "Kim, this towel is so cold."

"I know. Cold water makes you alert. It's time to tell it all."

Pam rubbed her face with the towel admitting to herself that it did awaken her some.

"Okay hun, you know it's not our intent to be flat out nosey, but it's important that you share with us what's been going on with you, because clearly you haven't been handling it well on your own," Monica said.

"You're right." Pam said fiddling with the cold towel in her hands.

Kim snatched the towel from Pam and threw it towards the kitchen.

"Kim stop being so insensitive." Monica said.

"Whatever. Come on Pam, especially after what I witnessed at work today, we need to know what's really been going on with you."

"Okay." Pam jumped up out of her seat and away from the ladies. She paced the floor for a second trying to figure out where to start her story.

Pam was hot. She remembered she still had her coat on. She took it off hanging it on the back of the high chair positioned at the island in the kitchen area. "Okay I'll tell you all everything, but no judgment right?"

They all turned their heads towards Renee staring her down.

"Hey, I can't help it if when I quote scriptures to you all, your convictions seems like judgment from me. Take that up with the Lord." Renee smirked.

They all laughed some shaking their heads at her.

"Okay, so I met him," Pam took a deep breath before saying the name she hadn't said in such a long time before earlier that day, "Steve, on my way home one day."

"I stopped by the grocery store to-"

There was a knock at the door.

Pam looked at her front door for a second but decided to ignore it assuming the person on the other side of the door must be at the wrong condo door in her building because no one else she knew had the gall to show up at her place unannounced.

"Like I was saying, I stopped by the grocery store to pick up a few groceries and some candy for my students for the next day. I was in the produce section when-"

The knocking at the door grew louder.

"Who is that at your door?" Kim didn't bother to let Pam answer the question as she walked towards it.

"Kim, what are you doing? Don't answer the door. I don't know who's there, and quite frankly, I don't care."

"Well I'm tired of the knocking interrupting your story. Who is it?" Kim looked through the peep hole. She stepped back and slowly pivoted to face Pam. She silently mouthed her words to Pam. "It's Mr. Sutherland."

"What? I can't hear you." Pam shouted down the hallway.

"I said, it's Mr. Sutherland." Kim now whispered.

"What?" Pam yelled as she walked down the hallway.

"Well since you ain't trying to be discreet, I won't either. I said, it's Mr. Sutherland."

Pam's eyes bucked as she covered her mouth. "Lower your voice."

"I was trying to do that all along."

Renee and Monica now stood in the entryway of the hallway leading to the front door. They waited to see what would unfold next.

"Why is he here?" Pam whispered to Kim.

"I don't know, beats me. Wait, how does he know where you live? Oh yeah, your personnel file." Kim noticed the shiftiness in Pam's demeanor. "Or has he been here before and that's why he's here, to check up on his woman?" Kim's hand was on her waist and her head was cocked to the side staring at Pam.

"No, it's nothing like that. He and I, there's nothing going on between us. He helped me move in. That's all."

"He was here before me?" Kim feigned being hurt by that knowledge. "Hmmph. A boss doesn't just show up at an employee's house after witnessing them in distress at work. They call, email, or wait to speak with them the next business day. They don't make house visits." Kim snapped her neck. "But this one does, so that tells me otherwise than what you're saying."

The knocking at the door continued, but this time it was aided by the gentle timber in his voice. "Ms.-Pam, it's me, Vance. I know I'm here unannounced, but you didn't answer your phone or respond to any of the messages I sent you. I need to know that you're okay?"

"Oh, that voice, there's definitely something going on with you two."

"Whatever, let me get rid of him so that I can get rid of you all too." Pam headed closer to the door.

"Tuh, you wish." Kim stepped aside for a second but then jumped back in front of the door grabbing Pam's hand from the knob. "You might wanna go check the mirror before you open the door."

"Shoot!" Pam remembered that she had been balling her eyes out earlier. She rushed to the bathroom by the front door. She gasped looking at her reflection. She looked like a raccoon. Her ruined mascara and eyeliner ran black tracks down her face. Her hair was extremely matted, but in the midst of her ugliness, she was grateful that her migraine had dissipated and she was left with a minor headache.

Kim came up behind her trying to pat her hair down as best as she could.

The knocking continued at the door. "Pam, I know you're in there and I won't leave until I see you…until I know you're really okay."

Pam shook her head. It was all too much for her to deal with now, but she reasoned that if she didn't come clean with the sisterhood that night and try to get Vance to leave her alone then the migraine's and her restless nights would continue.

She grabbed a makeup remover towelette from a pouch in the medicine cabinet and scrubbed her streaky face as best as she could. She turned to Kim, "how do I look?" She laughed.

Kim hesitated. "I guess you look aiight."

Pam smirked and pushed past Kim and headed to her front door. She put her hand on the knob but turned back to face Kim, "can you please give us some privacy?"

"You're asking too much now." Kim laughed. "I guess." Kim pouted as she walked down the hallway and stood next to the others.

Pam cocked her head and bucked her eyes at all of them. "I need privacy from all of you. Jeesh! Do something with yourselves."

The knocking continued at the door.

"How about you all start walking this way but make a right at the first open door. That's my bedroom. You can hang up some of my clothes for me in my closet. And close the door after you please. Thanks."

The women all stared at Pam with quizzical looks on their faces before they heeded to her request.

"The nerve. We came over here to support her emotionally but turn into her slaves." Kim griped.

She slammed the door to Pam's room after they were all in it.

Pam shook her head laughing a little. She patted at her hair again hoping it would magically be lustrous and kempt.

She put her hand on the door knob again but didn't twist it. She held her hand near her mouth and blew onto it. She was pleased that smell of her breath that entered her nostrils wasn't as horrid as she had looked moments ago in the mirror. She took a deep breath and finally opened the door.

Vance had his hand raised ready to knock on it again.

"You see me now? Do you see that I'm okay?" She threw her hands up in the air trying to smile.

Vance stared at her with his eyebrows almost touching each other. The sadness in her eyes tore at his heart. "No offense, but you don't look so okay."

She laughed. "None taken."

He shoved his hands in his pockets and leaned on her doorway. He stared deeply into her eyes.

She lowered her head averting further eye contact with him. His stare into her eyes always seemed to pierce her soul to its core.

"Are you really okay?" He said in a low voice.

"I'm fine."

"So will you look at me then?"

She looked up slowly into his eyes.

They gazed into each other's eyes for what seemed like an eternity before Vance broke the silence between them. "I know you want to keep things professional between us, but that's so hard for me because I…"

"Can you please try?"

"I'm trying, but you can't think that I could witness what I did today during and after that meeting and not be worried about you. Not care more for you." He let out a long breath.

Pam paused before speaking. "I'm sorry you had to witness that today."

"That, yes that. The way you cringed in your seat from what seemed like merely being in the same room with Asia's dad. And to come back in the room and hearing you tell him to back up and leave you alone but he didn't. I wanted to hurt him."

"I'm glad you didn't."

"I would have though." Vance's jaws tightened and his pupils danced with anger.

Pam smiled slightly. "But I'm glad you didn't." She reached out and rubbed his arm but immediately pulled it back feeling the kismet vibe between them.

He stood up straight and folded his arms at his chest. He looked down at her in such a loving manner.

She stepped back from him. What was between them blanketed her in an unexplainable way. She hoped the space she added between them would dissolve some of her interest in him at the moment.

He stepped closer to her. "May I come in?"

"I'm sorry, you can't. I have company."

"Oh, I didn't mean to intrude, but you weren't answering your phone. I had to know if you were safe and alright."

Pam saw the sincerity for her safety in his eyes and it gnawed at her heart.

"Yes, Mr.- Vance I'm okay."

"Good. So how do you and Steve know each other?" Vance immediately regretted saying the guy's name as he watched wrinkles form in Pam's forehead and the look of disgust in her eyes. He hated Steve for whatever he did to Pam, but he wanted to know what happened between Pam and Steve.

"Vance, clearly you won't let us," she pointed between herself and him, "just be strictly professional, and right now I'm too drained to try and assert myself with you like that. I suspect that you won't leave me or the situation alone until you have some type of knowledge about it. So, in a nutshell, he and I dated until I found out how worthless he really was, is."

Vance tried to speak, but Pam cut him off.

"I hate to be so short with you, but my best friends are here, and I know that if I don't get back to them ASAP, they will come out of my room and do a full interrogation of you and me. And trust me, you don't want that."

"I wouldn't mind discussing a you and I with them."

"Look, Vance, even if I weren't dealing with all of this other stuff on my plate, you know very well that you and I wouldn't be a good couple."

His eyebrows furrowed. "Why not?"

"Don't act like you don't know."

"I don't."

"We aren't equally yoked."

"Was it an equal 'yoke' when you were with him?"

Pam became furious with Vance. "Look, you have no right to-"

"Pam," he reached and grabbed her shoulders trying to calm her down but she pulled back from him seething with anger.

Vance continued, "I'm sorry. I didn't mean to say that. I wish that you would give us a chance."

"Please leave now." She stood with her eyes narrowed in on him, her arms folded at her chest and tapped her foot.

"I'm sorry. I didn't mean to upset you. Please forgive me. Can we talk about this?"

"Leave!" She pointed past him.

Kim, Monica, and Renee ran from the room to Pam's defense.

Vance saw Kim and would now have to add her to the list of employees who might avoid him at work for personal reasons; Pam being the only other one on the list he knew of.

"Okay. I'm sorry to upset you, but please know that I honestly didn't mean to offend you. I, I, I…"

he let his thoughts remain unsaid as he dropped his head and headed down the stairs. He knew he wouldn't win an argument with her and her friends that night.

"Are you okay?" Kim asked.

Pam slammed the door and fell against it. She tried sliding down it to the floor, but the ladies picked her up before she could reach the bottom.

"Oh no you won't. Get up. No more pity partying for you sister." Monica said propping Pam up and walking her down the hallway yet again.

"Whatever it is attacking you, we come against it right now." Renee was ready to pray.

Kim stopped and looked at Renee. "Mother Intercessor, since we don't know exactly what the issue with her is yet, how about you hold off on calling out spirits."

"What? Prayer is always in order." Renee looked at Kim.

"Yeah, yeah, I know that, but can you wait a second."

"My lips may not be praying now, but my spirit will continue to."

"Jee, thanks." Kim said sarcastically as she walked down the hallway. She went into the kitchen area and poured them all a glass of orange juice.

Renee and Monica resumed their positions on both sides of Pam.

Kim returned with orange juice for each of them. She sat down ready to finally listen to Pam's story. "Spill it now." She barked at Pam.

"Okay, but I honestly don't feel like giving you all the long version, so I'll abbreviate it."

"The hell you will."

"Kim!" Renee's mouth opened wide from shock, although how Kim spoke and behaved at times should never have come as a surprise to her.

"What. Oh excuse my language, but we haven't waited all of this time for the Dr. Seuss version of her story. Nope, I don't care if it takes all night, you will fill us in on all of what's been eating at you and that includes what's going on between you and Mr. Sutherland. Don't look surprised as if I haven't noticed the looks you all give each other. How much you two talked during the conference in Atlanta." She compressed her lips at Pam.

"Oh hush. Let me finish my story from earlier so I can put you all out and get some sleep. I don't think I'll make it in to work tomorrow."

"Good sweetie, you need to rest." Monica patted her knee.

"So, as I was saying earlier, I met," she took a deep breath, "Steve at the grocery store. I was looking for the milk I wanted and apparently he was checking for me." Pam held her hand up silencing Kim. "Either you keep your mouth closed and let me tell this story without any of your quips and sarcastic retorts, or I'll keep you all in the dark."

Monica and Renee shot "you better keep your mouth shut" looks at Kim.

She giggled as she pretended to zip her lips, lock them, and throw away the key.

Pam continued. "We introduced ourselves to one another. He smelled so good and he was so easy on the eyes." She scowled thinking about why they ended.

"Pam, it's okay." Renee said.

Pam came back to the moment and continued to talk. "Well, he walked with me around the store talking to me while I finished shopping. He was so easy to talk to. He asked me for my number and I gladly gave it to him. And from there everything seemed to move fast, but it seemed right until…"

"Until what?" Kim asked.

Monica stared Kim down and Kim quickly zipped her lips yet again.

"Until he started pressuring me to have sex."

"How long was that into dating him?" Monica asked.

Pam looked to Monica. "About three to four months into the relationship."

"Oh sweetie, I wish you would've shared this with us. We could've helped you get over him sooner than this. But what I don't get is that if you broke it off with him when he started pressuring you for sex, why are you still not over him now?" Monica asked.

"Why does Monica get to ask questions but I don't?" Kim pouted.

They all laughed.

Kim jumped up. "Wait a minute. Wait a minute. A woman is only distraught over a man like this after she gave it up to him. Oh Monica, boy do you have this one wrong."

"What?" Renee was confused.

"Sit down and shut it Sherlock Holmes." Pam jokingly demanded of Kim.

Kim obliged.

Renee finally understood Kim's implications. "Oh Pam, please don't tell me that you did have sex with him?"

Pam hung her head. "Yes, I did."

"Oh honey, you knew better than that. We're to wait until marriage. Our bodies belong to God." Renee said.

"Did you wait?" Pam cocked her head at Renee.

"You know I didn't. I can't take that back, but we all agreed not to go back to our sinful ways we behaved in college."

"No we all didn't agree to that." Kim said.

"Oh stop being silly, Kim." Renee said.

"Oh my naïve sister, I'm not being silly, I'm being serious. Whenever I do it, I enjoy it." Kim smiled.

"Kim. You know better than that." Renee said.

"But it's oh so good. I guess I don't get convicted the way y'all do." Kim said.

"Kim." Renee screamed.

Kim laughed.

"Ladies, let's finish listening to Pam." Monica said.

"Okay." Renee and Kim said in unison. Kim stuck her tongue out at Renee.

Pam continued. "Of course I believed that sex before marriage was wrong and I didn't want to do it but at the same time, I didn't want to lose him."

"Any man that won't accept your standards isn't the man for you sweetie." Monica said softly patting Pam's hand. "You know I learned that from experience."

"I know that, but at that time with the hustle and bustle of my work as a teacher and the stress of my master's classes, I didn't want to lose his companionship. I wanted a love of my own. I saw how happy you were with the twins and Keith." She looked to Monica. "You truly seem to enjoy being a social worker and in no rush for a man because God and your mission comfort you so." She looked at Renee. "And then there's you," she looked at Kim, "so carefree and foot loose. You're cool with or without a man. I guess I really felt like I needed him and it was better to give in to his one request than to be alone. I swear I resisted his advances for as long as I could until one night I gave in. In my head, to try and soothe my conscious, I reasoned that since he and I were going to get married, us doing it then wasn't all that bad."

"It was bad, but that's okay. You do know that He is faithful and just to forgive us of our sins and to cleanse us from all unrighteousness. God will forgive your fornicating ways if you ask Him sincerely with no intentions of doing it again."

"Yes, I know that King James." Pam snarled at Renee.

Renee pulled back some from Pam

"Okay sweetie, so if you've asked God for forgiveness and you know He gives it, why haven't you forgiven yourself and move on?" Monica inquired.

Pam lowered her head. Tears fell from her eyes.

They came in closer to her.

"It's okay. Let it out." Renee said.

Pam muffled through her tears. "Well after a month of having sex with him, he changed on me."

"How so?" Kim asked.

"I started seeing less and less of him. Before the sex, I would see him no more than four times out of the week. Of course I wanted to be with him every day, but with his job, he traveled a lot on the weekends."

"So what changed after y'all had sex?"

"I was questioning how little we had begun to see and talk to each other." Pam cried.

Renee ran to the bathroom and grabbed the box of Kleenex and handed it to Pam.

Pam grabbed the tissue, blew her nose, and wiped at her face.

"He sat there holding me telling me how much he loved me and that things between us would be better in time. Something didn't feel right to me about his responses for where he would be when not with me or at work. I jokingly said 'you act like you have a wife and a family somewhere else to take care of and spend time with.' He sat there silent and as stiff as ever. I jumped up out of the bed to get a good look at him and the look on his face told it all. He jumped out of the bed screaming he was sorry for not telling me about his wife and family from the beginning. He said things were so messed up at home and that he really cared for me, but he didn't want to tell me and I dismiss him before I got the chance to get to know the real him."

"The real him was a real jerk." Kim shouted.

"Okay. So you ended it that night, but you're still so torn over sleeping with a married man without knowing it?" Monica asked.

Pam sat silently.

"What else are you not telling us?" Kim scooted closer to Pam on the ottoman.

Pam wrung her hands tightly. "By that time in our relationship y'all, I was in love with him. I tried to put him out that night, but he wouldn't leave. He picked me up kicking and screaming and laid me on the bed. He kissed my body from head to toe. He kissed my tears away and then made love to me until I fell asleep under him."

"So you still had sex with him that night after he admitted to you that he was married?" Renee pulled away from Pam.

"Yes I did, Renee. I know it wasn't right, but I did that night and more nights after that." Pam hung her head.

Renee stood up. She walked over to the island in the kitchen area and sat on one of the stools.

"As a married woman, you know I can't condone your actions. To know he was married and still sleep with him was just plain wrong." Monica said.

"As Christian women, we can't condone any of her actions with the man." Renee said.

"No judgment remember?" Pam jumped up.

Renee spoke again. "It's not judgment honey, it's the truth, the Word of God. We don't have to say a thing about what you did and you would still be tormented inside as you have been. The Holy Spirit inside of you is calling you to make amends with what you've done." *I should know, I'm living it as we speak.*

"Don't you think I know that? Don't you think I've tried that?" Pam walked away from all of them.

"So why don't you feel better then?" Kim asked surprisingly bashful.

"Because I don't think God is listening to me. I don't think He will forgive me." Pam screamed out her last statement. "Like you said Monica, I was wrong. Not only did I give myself to a man who wasn't my husband, I defiled a marriage by sleeping with another woman's husband."

"No, he did that." Kim's nostrils flared.

"No, I played my part in that desecration too. The minute he told me he was married, I should've kicked him out and have been done with him, but no, I remained selfish. I ignored how my part in the affair would affect his family while I continued to sleep with him. I hate him for not telling me he was married, but I hate myself for breaking up his family."

"You can't and shouldn't carry that burden alone. He knew he was married when he stepped to you." Monica was fuming. She paced the floor back and forth.

"You don't really hate yourself, Pam. Let's go to God together. He makes all things new." Renee smiled.

"You don't get it. You all just don't get it." Pam threw her hands up in the air screaming.

They all stood silently staring at her.

Pam moved closer to them pointing her finger at each of them. "You just don't get it. I realized I hate myself today." She pointed to the floor. She sobbed but stifled her tears to speak anyway. "When I saw Steve come through that door today and introduced himself as Asia's dad, it hit me that I was the reason she had been acting out at school and bullying Sharday. Poor Sharday. Sharday has endured hell because of me."

"That's not true sweetie." Monica tried to reach out to Pam, but Pam jumped back from her.

"Yes it is. Whenever I spoke to Asia's mom, she would always say she thought Asia was acting out because her dad was no longer in the house with them and that they were getting a divorce. She said Asia had always been a daddy's girl and him not being there with her was messing her up."

"Pam-" Kim said.

"Don't Pam me. I don't care what y'all say, if I wouldn't have cheated with him, his wife would've never put him out. Asia would still have her dad at home and not have been so mean to Sharday all of this time. I set the events in motion that has Sharday hating herself and questioning why God made her the way he did. My adulterous ways created this mess." Pam was furious.

She raced over to the kitchen area rummaging through the drawers.

They all looked to one another.

Monica spoke up nervously. "Pam, sweetie, what are you looking for?"

"These!" Pam held up a pair of scissors. She had a determined look on her face.

They all took one step towards her.

"Oh don't worry, I'm not suicidal or homicidal, it's just time to make a change."

"What are you talking about?" Kim asked.

"That creep had the nerve to touch me today. He touched my hair talking about how soft it was, how he missed running his hands through it. Yada, yada, this and yada, yada that about my hair. It just hit me, he loved it and Sharday hates herself because she thinks my beauty is in my long and straight hair. Well, little do either of them know that I haven't had a relaxer in over two years. I flat iron it straight." She lifted the scissors. "I'll show them." She grabbed a big chunk of her hair and cut it off.

"Pam." They all screamed.

"Don't worry. I'm like India Arie, 'I am not my hair'." She grabbed another chunk of her hair and cut it off.

At least eight inches of hair fell to the floor that time.

"Pam, please put the scissors down." Renee's trembling voice pleaded.

"No. I'm fine. Since he loved my hair so much, I hope he thinks that I'm ugly with it gone if I ever see him again. Maybe then he'll leave me alone. And when Sharday sees me, I hope she can realize that beauty isn't found in the length or texture of a woman's hair, but what's on the inside of her. And thank God she doesn't know how ugly I am on the inside. I want her to be at peace with herself no matter how jacked up I am." Pam kept grabbing at her hair and cutting it until there were no long strands left to grasp.

Monica, Kim, and Renee stood there with their mouths covered. They tried hard to shield their amazement of the disaster Pam had created on her head. It looked like gum had gotten stuck in it, lots of it, and preschoolers took elementary scissors and helped Pam cut the glue out of her hair.

"Why are you all standing there looking at me like that? What, you don't like the way I look now? Did you all think my beauty was in my hair?" Pam patted the unevenness of her hair.

They began to step closer to her.

"No sweetie. You will always be beautiful." Kim reached out and grabbed Pam's wrist, took the scissors from her, and pulled her from the piles of her hair into her arms.

Monica and Renee huddled around them.

Pam tried to keep her stoic resolve for as long as she could before she finally broke down sobbing into Kim's arms.

They led her over to the couch and she collapsed on it.

"Why won't God hear my cry? Forgive me? Take this pain away from me?" Pam mumbled sobbing with her face buried in the couch.

"Pam, He's ready to forgive you sweetie. In fact, I'm sure He already has. Question is, are you willing and ready to forgive yourself?" Renee kneeled on the side of the couch and rubbed Pam's back trying to soothe her sobs.

"I've tried. It won't work."

"Even I see that you're ready to forgive yourself now." Kim said. She looked at Renee. "Now would be a good time for you to intercede."

They began to pray fervently for Pam as she cried out to God for forgiveness and the ability to forgive herself.

16

Vance sat in his car outside of Pam's house since she had put him out.

It was still winter, but his frayed emotions kept him from being concerned with his fogged windows and the circles of visible breath he was creating in the car. He was desperately trying to figure out why he seemed to keep putting his foot in his mouth where Pam was concerned. *Why do I even want her? It'll never work between us. She's a closed-minded Christian.*

He started up the car, but he didn't drive off yet, wondering if he should go back to her apartment and try to get her to hear him out again. He hated the way their conversation ended, and judging from the effects she had on him lately, he knew it would be a restless night for him if he didn't settle the tension between them before the night was over.

He gripped the keys in the ignition readying himself to take them out when his phone rang. *Maybe it's her.* He looked at his phone disappointed that it was only his brother calling him.

"Yeah?" Vance tried to sound cheerful.

"Meet me at the spot now." Marcus demanded of Vance before hanging up.

"And hello to you too." Vance looked at the phone as if Marcus could see the bewildered look on his face.

Vance knew the exact spot Marcus was talking about. They had been playing basketball at that same neighborhood gym since they were little boys.

It was a weeknight and Vance was distraught from his run in with Pam and could use the one on one match with his brother to relieve some of the tension in his body. Luckily, he always kept his gym bag in the trunk of his car, so he headed straight to the gym to meet his brother, Marcus.

When he made it there, he walked in and nodded at the usual night crew at the desk as he swiped his card.

"Hey, Vance." Charlene, the vibrant young woman at the desk, greeted him. She was relentless with flirting with him. Not discreetly, but overt with him all of the time, and that turned him off.

"Hey," he mumbled politely and kept walking past her. Although she was a very attractive woman to him, he knew of at least five other men that she had been involved with that frequented the gym. That was another thing about her that turned him off; he wasn't one to share.

Vance headed into the locker room. He slipped into his basketball shorts, shirt, and shoes and locked his things in the locker as he tried to recount where he went wrong with Pam that night.

He exited the locker room and headed to the court area. The court was empty except for Marcus already there and sweaty from doing some drills.

Vance walked towards his brother secretly admiring Marcus's skills on the court, but he would never admit that to him. They were rivals where basketball was concerned. Vance cleared his throat. "Why'd you call me demanding to meet you here tonight without even saying hi to me or asking me about my day before you hung up? I have feelings too." Vance laughed as he took a defensive stance in front of Marcus charging to the basket. "Where are the rest of the guys?" Vance looked around as if they would magically appear.

Marcus dribbled the ball on his right side knowing Vance was weak on his left side.   "We need to talk with them not around." Marcus said.

"And you couldn't have talked to me about whatever you want to talk about on the phone? You could have at least come to my house with some dinner for us to talk over, you know I love your wife's cooking. I'm hungry. I haven't eaten all day. Forget ball, let's go back to your house." Vance laughed and walked towards the door.

"I know you love her cooking, you eat up all the food whenever you're over there, but for this convo, we need to be on neutral territory. I don't want my kids and wife to hear or witness your ugliness about the topic." Marcus sniggered.

"What?" Vance inquired.

"You know what." Marcus said as he pointed to Vance.

Vance walked back towards Marcus staring him down. "If you wanna talk about what I think you wanna talk about, then I'm out." Vance said as he got in Marcus' face.

"You better back up and take some of that bass out of your voice talking to me like that before I beat you like daddy used to." Marcus demanded.

"Don't mention him." Vance shouted.

"I can talk about him whenever I want to. That's how I got over what happened to him, man. Don't you see how holding it in all of these years is killing you, man? You never grieved properly."

"Well I ain't dead yet." Vance retorted.

"Yes you are man. You died inside the day we found out dad had been murdered."

17

"Now that you remember who and whose you are, let's do something with this hair girl." Renee laughed as she tried to run her hands through Pam's hair.

"Yes, please. I hate to be the bearer of bad news, but girl, you look a mess. I mean something awful. You look like Edward Scissorhands got a hold of you. I mean you look a hot mess on a hot summer night." Kim smirked.

"Okay Kim, I think she got the message." Monica laughed as she shook her head.

"I'm just saying." Kim laughed.

"Whatever." Pam laughed as she got up off the couch. "Y'all don't know how much I love y'all and thank God for y'all standing in the gap and interceding on my behalf. Y'all prayed me through my own condemnation. I know I got my breakthrough after all of that praying and crying that we just did. My God that was so needed. I feel like a burden has been lifted off of my shoulders." Pam stood up jumping. "Y'all don't know how light I feel." She smiled.

The ladies knew it was Pam's moment to praise God. They each inwardly prayed that she would maintain the joy they saw in her at that time.

"No more condemnation for me. Thank you God." Pam clapped her hands. "I won't allow the mistakes and sins of my past to keep me from loving myself and experiencing the abundant life that You promised me God. Woooo! I feel so good."

Renee prayed in tongues as she cried tears of joy for Pam's deliverance.

"I pray for those that despitefully use me. If I see Steve again, I won't crumble at the sight of him. I'll pray for him. I pray that he comes in right relationship with the loving God that I serve. He has no effect on my emotions anymore. I'm free y'all."

Pam danced and praised God down the hall to the bathroom. "I gotta pee."

They all laughed at her last statement.

"Aaahhhh!"

"What?" Kim said as Monica and Renee followed her running down the hall to see why Pam screamed.

"Why did y'all let me do this to my head? I look a mess." She grabbed at her hair. "My eyes are red and puffy with a stuffy nose, I really look a mess." Pam laughed uncontrollably. The others joined in with her.

They left out of the bathroom locked arm in arm as best as they could down the hallway together.

"I am so hungry." Pam said.

"Who you telling?" Kim responded.

They continued laughing as they reentered the common area.

Monica's phone rang. She rushed to answer it.

"Yes Keith, I'm still here. How are my babies?...Okay... I'll be home soon."

"Oh Monica, I'm sorry. You've been here all of this time with me and you have a husband and babies you should be home with." Pam rushed to Monica's side.

"She's the only one you're apologizing to for taking up their time? Tuh." Kim poked out her lips.

Pam rolled her eyes and laughed as she looked at Kim. "I appreciate all of you for laboring with me until I got my breakthrough from God. I'm hungry and I'm sure you all are too. I would say that I would order some pizza and we talk more or you all could help me unpack some more, but I guess it is late." Pam gave them all the side-eye. "I could eat and unpack some more on my own."

"Whatever, you know we're all hungry and will stay and help you. Besides, my babies are in good hands with their father and then I'll be in his good hands when I get home." Monica winked.

"Again, eww. Mon, would you stop hinting at what you do with our brother?" Kim said. She looked at Renee, and the two of them shook their shoulders and heads as if being disgusted by the thought of their brother having sex.

Kim turned her attention to Pam. "Are you going to work tomorrow?"

"Yes."

"Well then, I ain't leaving til' you do something with that head of yours. It's too late to go to a shop now, and none will be open in the morning before you clock in at work. Girl, matter of fact, you need to call off of work tomorrow and go get that butchered mane of yours professionally tended too. Good God girl, your head looks a mess." Kim flopped back onto the couch and propped her feet up on the ottoman.

"Whatever, jerk." Pam stuck her tongue out at Kim. "If Renee doesn't mind, between her and I, we can have my head looking right until I can get to my stylist after work."

Renee nodded her head in agreement.

"I can't miss tomorrow. I have to be there for Sharday. I want to show her my natural hair, help her to see our hair doesn't define us, it's what's in our hearts that does."

"Well alright Sister Soldier." Kim pumped her fist in the air. "I don't care if you relax it tonight, rock a fro, or whatever, you better make sure that it's neat tomorrow, unlike how it is now."

"Whatever. Let me order the pizza so that it can be on its way, while Renee gets started on my head. You and Monica can hang up some clothes for me."

"Do I look like a maid to you? Tuh. I'm here for entertainment purposes at this point." Kim tightened her lips.

Pam cocked her neck. "I may look a mess for now, but you *are* a mess." Pam threw a throw pillow at Kim as she laughed.

Kim covered her face to shield it from the pillow as she laughed.

Pam ordered pizza while Renee readied the flat irons. Monica busied herself in Pam's master closet hanging up clothes.

Kim sat relaxed on the couch checking her Instagram account.

"Well, you non-maid, you can stay in here if you want but it looks like the party is moving to my room." Pam stuck her tongue out at Kim as she turned off the lights in the kitchen and common area and headed to her room.

"It's okay. I was in the dark about your life this past year, a few moments of sitting in here in the dark now won't hurt me one bit."

Pam and Kim laughed hysterically as Pam left, but Kim sat in the dark checking the comments on some of her pics on Instagram. She joined them in the bedroom minutes later.

She walked in and scanned the room for the best spot for her to get comfy in. Luckily for her, Monica was using a chevron printed oversized arm chair as a workstation while she hung the clothes instead of using the bed as many others would have. She flopped down on the bed and it grabbed a hold of her, comforting her.

"Pam?"

"What?"

"This bed, I love it."

"Silly, don't call my name like that unless you really want something."

"I do, this bed. Where did you get it from?"

"I'll tell you when I locate the receipt."

"Do that soon, please? Meanwhile, I'll sleep in it and you can sleep in one of your guest rooms." Kim laughed as she hugged the equally plush pillows close to her body. "Man you are so selfish for not inviting us, especially me, over sooner."

"Why, so you could've met my bed sooner?"

"Exactly."

Pam hit Kim on her leg playfully.

The doorbell rang.

"Must be the pizza man. Anybody putting in on this pizza with me?" Pam held her hand out and scanned the room waiting for them to place some money in her hands.

They all turned their backs to her as if they couldn't hear her.

"Whatever." Pam laughed. "I guess I could treat you all this time." She laughed and went in search of her purse.

The doorbell rang again.

"Kim, would you buzz the door to let him in while I find my purse? Thanks."

"But I don't wanna move. I may not find this exact spot of comfort when I come back in here." Kim whined.

"I hate when that happens too." Renee laughed as she readied her makeshift hair station to do Pam's hair.

"Please?" Pam called out from the kitchen.

"Okay, okay, okay. You don't have to beg me."

Monica and Renee shook their heads at Kim and laughed as Kim left the bedroom.

Kim buzzed the pizza guy in and then stood at the door with it opened waiting for him or Pam to appear first. She didn't care who appeared first; she was concerned about getting back to that exact comfy spot on the bed.

The delivery guy and Pam made it to the door at the same time. Kim was in shock that Pam so willingly stood there talking to him looking in such disarray. He didn't seem alarmed or turned off by her frazzled looks either. He smiled at her before speaking. "That'll be thirty dollars." The young man said in his deepest voice possible. He looked Pam straight in her eyes.

She handed him two twenty-dollar bills.

He gave her a sly smile and a wink as he handed her the pizza. "Wait, let me give you your change."

"Oh no, you keep it." She smiled oblivious to his flirting.

"Thanks." He winked at her.

Pam spoke while closing the door. "No problem. Enjoy the rest of your night."

The delivery guy stood on the other side of the door. He had worked up the courage to ask her out, but she had gently closed the door in his face before his lips parted.

"What was that?" Kim asked.

"What was what?" Pam said.

"The delivery guy was flirting with you and you didn't respond to it at all. And might I add, with the way your head looks, I'm not sure why he was interested in you at all." Kim laughed.

They walked back into Pam's bedroom.

Monica continued to fold and hang clothes quietly staying out of what she hoped wouldn't become an argument between Kim and Pam. She admitted to herself that although she knew Kim was joking and loved each of them, Kim's sarcastic comments could be hurtful at times when thrown back to back at whoever she was speaking to.

"Enough already with the jokes about my hair." Pam spoke to Kim. "Renee is about to hook me up right now." Pam smiled at Renee. "Aren't you?"

Renee smiled and nodded her head.

"Well forget about your head, all I'm saying is that you should've flirted back with him. He looked like he wanted to say more, but you practically slammed the door in his face before he could say anything." Kim grabbed a paper plate and napkins from the stack that Pam had placed on her dresser.

"If he was flirting with me, it wouldn't have mattered anyway because he's not my type. I don't want to get involved with anyone right now." Pam grabbed a few slices of pizza before she sat down under Renee so that Renee could work her magic with the scissors, comb, and flat irons near her. "Want some?" Pam held a slice of pizza up to Renee's lips.

Renee laughed. "No, I'll wait until I finish your hair before I eat. Thanks though." Renee smiled.

Kim plopped down on the bed with a slice of pizza in her hand. She stared at Pam. "And who *is* your type, Vance?" Kim tightened her lips.

Monica's ears perked up at the sound of Vance's name. They had heard the end of him and Pam's not so friendly conversation. Monica didn't know as much about him as Kim did, so she was eager to learn more about him if he seemed to rile Pam up the way he did. There had to be something there between them.

Monica came out of the closet, grabbed a plate and some pizza and sat on the bed facing Pam.

The attention seemed to be back on her, so she spoke up.

"Ladies, knowing that I just got my breakthrough from dealing with Steve, why would you all even think or try to encourage me to try something with Vance?" Pam rolled her eyes as she bit into her cheesy pizza. She smiled with her head low.

"Because like you said, you're free of Steve, so now you can explore other options, and from the looks of it, Vance is an option." Kim licked her lips.

"Have you no shame?" Renee shook her head.

They all laughed.

"Nope." Kim laughed chomping on her pizza.

"I hate to burst your bubble Kim, but Vance isn't an option either." Pam frowned inwardly admitting to herself that she was attracted to him.

"Why not?" Monica asked.

She sat silent for a moment. "I don't want to share his business, but, he doesn't believe in God."

"What do you mean a fine black man like him doesn't believe in God?" Kim gawked.

Renee shook her head at Kim.

"What? I know it's 2015, but it's still hard to believe hearing about a black person that does not believe in my Lord and Savior." Kim placed her hand over her chest feigning being dismayed of the news.

"Sometimes I wonder if you believe in God the way you carry on." Renee mumbled to herself.

"I heard you missy. But because I'm not as an uptight Christian as you are doesn't mean that I'm not a Christian." Kim rolled her eyes.

"Christian means Christ-like and sometimes you act nothing like Him." Renee stared down Kim.

"You better be glad I'm digging into Pam's life right now, otherwise, I would get on you about your last statement, but I'mma let it slide for now. But remember, I know where you live." Kim zoomed her stare in on Renee.

"You are nuts." Monica laughed turning to look at Kim.

"Anywho, no more about me. Pam, are you serious, our boss is an atheist?" Kim came to sit on the floor on the plush gray carpet near Pam.

"Yup, he said there's no reason for him to believe in a God like ours."

"What?" Monica was saddened and confused by that statement.

"I'm gonna definitely pray for him." Renee chimed in.

Pam threw something at Kim to get her undivided attention. "You better not say anything about it to him."

"I'm not crazy, I won't. He's still my boss and I don't want things to be awkward between he and I. Shoot, I hope it won't be since I witnessed the spat between you two earlier." Kim bit into more of her pizza.

"All I know is that 2 Corinthians 6:14 says, 'Do not be unequally yoked...' Amos 3:3 also questions two people walking together successfully in life unless they agree. If God is telling me to stay clear of someone like Vance, then I'mma take heed. I didn't listen to his instructions last time about not having sex before marriage and that caused my heart a world of pain. I'm done not listening to God."

"But I can tell that you really like Vance, Pam." Kim was serious.

"In the words of Tina Turner, what's like got to do with it?"

Confusion sculpted Renee's face as she spoke. "Wait, she didn't say like, she said love."

The others laughed at her.

"I know what the song says, but you get my drift." Pam said. She smelled the heat from the flat irons and it prompted her to speak up. "Thanks for evening out my hair some Renee, but I don't want it flat ironed." She jumped up and rushed to her master bath to look in the mirror. She grabbed her hair before speaking again. "All of the relaxed hair seems to be cut off, so I want to rock my natural curls and show Sharday tomorrow that my black is beautiful."

They all looked at her wide-eyed.

18

Pam woke up the next morning refreshed thanking God for freeing her from herself and blessing her to see another day.

Although she had never worn her hair that short before, she kind of liked the afro look on herself. Granted, her curl pattern was a little bit looser than that of the average afro sported during the 1970s, she knew her natural look would drive home the idea of "loving the skin you are in" to Sharday.

She played with her hair in the mirror until her curls framed her face to her liking. She left her house in search of a great day.

She arrived to school later than what she normally did, so all of the office staff were present as opposed to her normally being there before them.

She walked in wearing joy as her fragrance.

Shelly, the school clerk, spoke up first. "Ms. Robinson, your hair." Shelly walked over to Pam at the time clock. "Can I touch it?"

Pam laughed. "Sure."

"I love it. Girl, I think you can rock any hairstyle. I liked your long straight hair on you, but girl, I love this." She patted Pam's hair one more time before returning to her desk.

Others around the office continued to compliment Pam on her new look as she checked her mailbox.

They cackled laughing at some of the pics Shelly had pulled up on the computer as they discussed the comeback of natural hairstyles and all of the different shapes and colors it was in this time around.

"Well you guys, it was fun going back down memory lane with you all, but I need to get up to my classroom and prepare for the day." Pam said backing out of the office with her hands full.

"Okay. See ya later." Shelly said to Pam but quickly resumed her conversation about hairstyles with the rest of the office staff.

Pam walked up the stairs with her hands full of bags of supplies that she needed to replenish some things around her classroom.

She walked slowly wondering where Vance was. Although she normally was the first teacher in the building every morning, Vance would be there when she got there. She would've sworn that he would have come out of his office while the hair commotion was going on, but he didn't. She remembered she didn't see his car in the parking lot either. She shook off her worry of him not being there assuming he was simply running late and that she would see him later on during the school day.

Pam entered her classroom and put on some inspirational music causing her to dance as she went about her morning preparing before the kids came.

She was saddened by the bell ringing signaling the kids would need to be picked up meaning she had to pause her praise party, but she remembered that she had four bedrooms, three bathrooms, and a beautiful big common area in her condo that she could dance in when she got home that evening.

She went and stood in the hallway and waited for the kids to come up.

They gawked at her as they walked past her.

"Ms. Robinson, what did you do to your hair?" Michael asked.

The boys behind him laughed, but he turned to them and stared them down daring them to continue laughing at his favorite teacher.

The other boys stifled their laughter immediately.

"Well, Michael, I cut it."

"Why'd you do that?" He asked as he stood by her in the hall.

"Let's say it was necessary." Pam smiled.

"I guess." Michael shrugged his shoulders and left her standing in the doorway of the class to go put his things in his locker.

Soon, all of Pam's students were in the classroom completing their morning exercises.

Pam gave them the chance to chat what they thought was to themselves to discuss her hair change. She knew it was a shock to them and they needed this time to adjust to her new look. Although she had only been there with them for a while, she had built a strong bond with her class as a whole, and as with any family, anytime there is change with one member, it may take time for the other members to adjust.

She was taking attendance when Sharday came in late.

Sharday scanned the room looking for Pam. When she didn't see her, she leaned down and whispered to the student nearest her. "Where's Ms. Robinson today? Is she sick?"

"No silly. That's her at her desk." Another normally quiet girl in the class answered Sharday.

"Unh un. That ain't her. Ms. Robinson has long pretty straight hair."

"Well not anymore." The girl snickered.

"Stop playing. That's not Ms. Robinson." Sharday whispered in amazement.

Pam continued responding to an email on her computer with her back turned to where Sharday stood.

"That's her. Look. Ms. Robinson?" The girl called out.

"Yes." Pam turned to see which student called her. She smiled heartily when she saw Sharday standing next to Brianna.

"Brianna, what is it sweetie? Sharday, I see you finally made it to school. Do you have a tardy pass for me?"

"Never mind." Brianna giggled watching Sharday walk slowly towards Pam with her eyes bulging beyond their sockets and her mouth wide open.

Sharday stopped arm's length short of Pam and handed her the note from the office. "My momma's car wouldn't start. That's why I'm late."

"It's okay, Sharday. What matters is that you made it here safely."

"Ms. Robinson…"

Pam smiled knowing why Sharday was in such shock.

"Hurry and put your things away." She winked at Sharday and turned her attention to the rest of her students. "Okay class, clean your areas and when I see that you're ready I'll call tables to line up for art."

The kids enjoyed making things with their hands so much that an immediate silence fell over the classroom. They all wanted to get down to the art room as soon as possible to have as much time as they could to work on the sculptures they were making in art.

"Okay, you all can line up quietly now." Pam smiled as they each quietly fell in their proper places in line.

She walked her class to the art room. Ms. Spindel stood at the door waiting to greet the students. She spoke to each one of them as they entered her room.

Sharday stood at the back of the girls' line as usual.

"Ms. Spindel, I'm going to keep Sharday with me if that's okay with you?"

"Yes. Is everything okay?" Ms. Spindel asked with concern. She really did care about her students.

"Oh yes, everything's fine. She's not in trouble. I just need to talk to her about some things."

"Okay then. Well, Sharday, I hope you enjoy your time with Ms. Robinson." Ms. Spindel smiled and closed the door to her room behind her.

"Do you want to go back to my room with me to talk?" Pam said warmly to Sharday.

"Sure." Sharday mumbled.

Pam and Sharday walked back to the classroom in silence.

Pam walked past the main office and peeked in but she saw or heard no sign of Vance. She frowned admitting to herself she was disappointed in not having seen him yet.

Pam unlocked her classroom door and allowed Sharday to walk in front of her.

Sharday walked in the room and headed towards her seat.

"Sharday, where are you going?"

"To my desk." She never looked back at Pam.

"I didn't bring you up here to sit at your desk. I wanted to talk to you about yesterday and some other stuff. Come sit up here with me." Pam's cheerful voice reached Sharday's ears.

Sharday smiled a little as she went and sat next to Pam at her desk. She sat with her head down and fiddled with her hands.

Pam sighed. "Sharday, you have to learn to look people in the face when talking to them."

Sharday lifted her head but still refused to make eye contact with Pam.

"Okay, so how are you feeling about yesterday?"

Sharday looked up at Pam with a slight smile on her face. "I feel ok. Good, I guess."

"Oh good." Pam clapped her hands smiling.

Sharday laughed under her breath.

"And what about yesterday made you feel as good?"

Sharday continued to play with her fingers but made intermittent eye contact with Pam. "I don't know, I guess the fact that Asia took down all of the awful memes about me and deleted all of the negative posts of me." Sharday lowered her head and smiled.

Pam smiled. "Well, that's great. You should be happy."

"Yeah, and she said hi to me on my Facebook wall last night, which made other kids in the class say hi to me too." Sharday now smiled exposing all of her teeth.

"So all of this is good, right? You can just be a kid now, right?"

Sharday sat up in her seat and stared Pam in her eyes. "But what if this isn't over with them? What if they go back to being mean to me tomorrow?" Sharday dropped her head in her hands on the desk.

Pam tried to contain her laughter but she couldn't help herself. Her conversations with Sharday lately reminded her of the afterschool specials that aired on TV in the 80s and 90s where the focus was on teaching the youth on the show how to handle certain social situations that were ailing them "Sharday," she grabbed Sharday's chin to lift her head up, "you can't, nor, should you worry yourself with what may happen. Enjoy your today. Maybe they really have learned to be better towards you. Let's stop worrying about stuff that may not happen." She winked at Sharday.

"Okay, I'll try."

"Good, but why are you still frowning?"

"They may be nice to me now, but I'm still ugly and I hate my hair."

"Sharday, how many times do I have to stand you in front of that mirror and show you how beautiful you are?"

"It wouldn't matter how many times you do it, I'd still see myself as ugly. I'm not pretty like you. You cut your hair short and it's still pretty and all curly," Sharday reached over and pulled on one of Pam's curls. "My hair's been short and nappy all of my life. I'm as black as tar. I hate the way I look."

Pam prayed inwardly that God would give her the right words to say to get through to Sharday.

"Come on, I guess we need some mirror time again." Pam said.

Sharday laughed as Pam dragged her over to the mirror in her closet.

Pam stood behind Sharday forcing Sharday to look in the mirror at herself.

Sharday looked briefly into the mirror but lowered her head again. She refused to look at herself at first but eventually succumbed to doing so after Pam's persistent tickling of her sides and cheeks.

"Okay Ms. Robinson, I'm looking at myself, but I don't see what you see. You say I'm beautiful, but I think you're talking about you when you look in the mirror." A tear escaped Sharday's eye.

"Sharday, I'm standing here looking at two very beautiful black women in this mirror. You know what?"

"Hunh?"

"It's a choice for us daily to see the beauty in ourselves. I make that choice daily despite what I've gone through or may go through."

Sharday's eyebrows raised with curiosity of what Pam's life was like outside of being a teacher.

"My hair has always been long and I loved to wear it straight. I cut it last night on a whim, in an emotional state that I was unfamiliar with. I wasn't worried about how it would look when I cut it. I could only laugh at myself of how I looked after I cut it." Pam drew in a deep breath and laughed a little recounting the night before.

"But it looks good on you." Sharday frowned.

"I didn't know how it would turn out in the end or even cared for that matter. You know, when I cut it, I called myself getting back at someone."

Sharday's eyes shifted from side to side, her eyebrows furrowed.

Pam smirked. "Don't worry about who, nosey."

They both laughed. "Anywho, after I had cut it and before I looked at it, I thought about you."

"You did?" Sharday's eyes widened.

"Yep, I sure did. I laughed thinking you thought my hair was so straight and silky smooth, but the truth of the matter is I only get relaxers twice a year. I keep it conditioned and flat ironed to make it straight. So when I cut my hair, I essentially cut off the relaxed hair and was left with my natural curls. Cutting my hair turned out to be a good thing."

"How so?"

"I figured that I could show you that our black is beautiful no matter what." Pam raised her hand to high-five Sharday.

Sharday laughed and responded to Pam with a weak high-five.

"Come on Sharday." Pam grabbed Sharday's shoulders and shook her as if she was trying to shake Sharday into a better state of mind. "I need you to see how beautiful you are. I woke up this morning, looked in the mirror and realized that my beauty wasn't tied to the length or the straightness of my hair and I need you to see that your beauty isn't lacking because your hair is short and curled tighter than anyone else's. I wish you could see you the way I see you, better yet, the way God sees you. You are fearfully and wonderfully made in His eyes. He formed you in your mother's womb before the foundation of the earth. You *are* as He wanted you to be. God doesn't make mistakes and He does all things well. Sharday, you *are* gorgeous." Pam choked on her last words as the tears streamed her face. She pulled Sharday into a motherly embrace.

Sharday whimpered softly while Pam prayed over her.

They finally pulled apart from one another and wiped the tears from their faces.

Sharday turned around and faced the mirror again. She rid her face of any trace of having just cried. She leaned in closer to the mirror and pulled her mouth open by pulling on the corners of it to playfully expose all of her teeth. "I guess I kind of have a pretty smile." She laughed.

She leaned in even closer to the mirror smoothing out her eyebrows. "I guess the slant of my eyes are right for my face." She looked back at Pam and laughed some more.

She leaned in even closer to the mirror. "I guess my big nose matches my pretty smile and my slanted bright eyes."

She leaned in even closer to the mirror and pulled on her hair. "I guess the color of my hair and the length goes with the shape of my eyes and nose, the prettiness of my smile, and matches the color of my dark skin. I guess, I just might be pretty after all." She laughed and cried at the same time. "Thank you Ms. Robinson." She faced Pam and hugged her tightly.

"You are so welcome, pretty girl. Here's a book for you to read about how God sees you, so if you ever question yourself again, read a page or two then stare yourself down in the mirror until you see your beauty again."

"Thanks." Sharday smiled taking the book from Pam and holding it close to her.

"Now let's clean our faces and go pick up the rest of the students."

They both laughed.

Pam sent Sharday to the bathroom to wash her face while she remained in front of the mirror in the classroom patting her eyes and reapplying her lip gloss. She was happy that Sharday seemed to have gotten the truth of her being beautiful, but she was still remiss by not having seen Vance yet that day.

She went down to the first floor and slowly walked past the main office hoping to get a glimpse of him in there, but stopped in her tracks in the hallway at the mention of his name. Shelly, the clerk, was speaking to Barb, the business manager. "Girl, Mr. Sutherland never misses a day, but he called saying that he won't be in today. Something must really be wrong with him."

"Well how did he sound?"

"He didn't sound sick, he sounded sad, but what do I know. I hope he's okay."

"Yeah, me too."

"Anyway girl, did you see Scandal last night, girl…" Shelly said.

He sounded sad? Pam wondered if their altercation the night before caused his absence at work that day. For as much as she wished he hadn't popped up at her house the night before, looking back on it, she realized his concern for her pushed him to show up at her place unannounced. And although she didn't want anything romantic with him, as she was trying to convince herself, they honestly had been on the track to a good friendship. *Maybe I should try to check up on him after work. But wait, I don't have his address, but I do have his number. Should I try and call him now? Ugh! Now this is gonna plague my thoughts all day.*

***

It was now Pam sitting in her car outside of Vance's house.

She called him after work but he didn't answer, so she left a voicemail. She texted him as well, but he didn't respond to any of her texts. She couldn't leave well enough alone, so she managed to get his home address from Shelly the clerk. She questioned if she was doing the right thing all the way to his house, but for some innate reason, she couldn't do anything but follow the directions GPS outlined through her car speakers. She reasoned that since she was there now she might as well brave it out and go up to his door and speak to him. She knew he was there or at least he should be seeing as though his Mustang was in his driveway. She took a deep breath, turned off the engine, and got out of her car.

Traces of snow still scattered the ground. She looked down tracking her steps as she walked to make sure she wouldn't be the victim of falling on any black ice. She let out a deep sigh of relief when she made it to the front door without falling. She let her eyes scale up the tall stature of his brick home. Judging from the landscaping and what she could see of his décor through his curtain-less windows, he had great taste. She was enamored with the rich earth tones that blended so well together from where she stood.

She mustered up all the courage she could and rang his doorbell. She stepped back hoping that he wouldn't open it and it would free her from having to apologize to him for her rudeness the night before, if that was what kept him from work that day. She stood there for a minute, rang the doorbell again but surmised that maybe he wasn't home. Since he still hadn't come to the door, it was simply too cold outside for her to stand there any longer. She pivoted on her heels and walked back towards her car shoving her gloved hands into her Peacoat pockets.

"Pam? Is that you?" Vance called out with a mixture of surprise and happiness in his voice.

She slowly turned around to see him standing in his doorway. She noticed he was shivering, so she rushed her steps towards his front door again. She stopped an arms-length short of him becoming shy in front of him.

"Hi." She looked at him but then quickly looked away from him fidgeting with her car keys in one pocket and an old gum wrapper in the other.

"What brings you here?" He stared cautiously at her.

She stammered as she spoke. "Well, I, I, I wanted to come and check up on you."

He smirked.

"Things ended between us badly last night and honestly with what I was going through at the time that didn't matter. But when I got to the school this morning, I noticed you weren't there," she looked at the ground rather than looking at him, "and then I overheard Shelly tell someone else in the office that you sounded sad and whatnot on the phone." She still refused to look him in the eyes but looked past him into his house. "It had me wondering."

He laughed some at her constantly avoiding eye contact with him. "Would you like to come in? It's pretty cold out here. I'm shivering and I see that you are too."

"No, I, I, I don't want to intrude on your personal space."

"Trust me, you won't be."

"Okay."

Vance stepped aside and allowed Pam to enter his home.

He closed the door behind him. "You were wondering what?"

Pam thought what she saw of his house through the window was beautiful, but she was in complete awe of his twenty-four foot high ceilings with the rustic décor. *I wonder if a woman helped him decorate.* The more Pam looked around his home from where she stood the more her eyebrows furrowed. She was jealous at the thought of another woman sharing his space with him. She laughed.

"What's funny?"

"Hunh?" Pam realized Vance was talking to her.

"You came in saying you wondered something but never finished your thought and now you've been standing here scanning my house and then you laugh. Fill me in." Vance was amused as he stared at her.

She looked him in his eyes. "I'm sorry, I wasn't laughing at you or your house, I was laughing at a silly thought in my head."

"Okay." He shrugged his shoulders giving up on trying to find out what caused her smile and faint but sweet laughter invade his thoughts minutes earlier. "Want me to take your coat and hat?"

"No, I don't want to impose on your time any longer. I know I showed up unannounced and all." Pam looked away.

Vance smiled.

"Pam, let me take your coat and hat. We can sit down and talk over some hot chocolate or whatever you'd like to drink."

"Okay, maybe I can stay for a minute, just a minute." She cocked her head to the side and smiled at him with her eyes as she wagged one finger in his face.

He laughed. "I gotchu."

She took off her knitted hat and put it in the sleeve of her peacoat before she handed it to him.

Vance stood there speechless staring at her.

Pam looked up and noticed the keen look of shock and admiration in Vance's eyes. "What?" She laughed.

"Your hair?" He stepped back and draped her coat over the coat rack at the front door.

"What about it?" She followed him into the sunken den and right in front of the fireplace.

"It's different. I love it. I mean, I like it. It looks great on you. It compliments your eyes, your face, you." He smiled at her and stepped back to get a better look at her hair, at her.

She was inwardly glad that he liked her new look, but she became uncomfortable under his intense stare of her. *This was a mistake coming here.* She jumped back up to her feet. "Look, I think I should leave now."

"No, don't go." He cupped his hands together almost in a prayer-like position.

"No, I should. The only reason I came over was because you didn't respond to my texts and emails today nor did you answer my calls at all today. You're my boss and after all that I said to you yesterday and the way that I said it, I wanted to apologize. No hard feelings?" She extended her hand out to him to shake his as if declaring a truce between the two of them.

He grabbed her hand. He held it for a minute as they talked with their eyes. He ended the conversation their eyes, their souls were having with his words. "Don't go. Sit back down and let's talk some more."

She snatched her hand from his loosening the currents of interest that flowed freely between them. "I can't stay. I shouldn't have come here unannounced. I needed to know that I wasn't the reason why you didn't come to work today when you love what you do."

He reached back out for her hand, but she turned her back and made her way to the stairs. "I would like my coat and hat, please." She stood at the front door waiting for him to meet her there.

He handed her the coat. "Pam, my reason for not being at work today had nothing to do with you. It's something else I'm dealing with and I needed time away from everyone and everything. That's why I didn't answer your calls or respond back to your texts and emails earlier. I wasn't in the right headspace and I didn't want to say the wrong thing to you." He looked deep into her eyes as he stepped closer to her. "Clearly you thought I was out of order last night. I didn't want to say or do anything else to further distance you from me."

She wanted to put more distance between them, but his eyes wouldn't let her. She continued to stare into them. Her mouth was dry, but she spoke in a low, soothing tone. "We both may have been out of line last night. In hindsight, I know you were there to check up on me given how I fled from work yesterday. That's why I had to return the favor today of checking up on you. I apologize for being so rude to you last night."

"No need to apologize. I'm the one who's sorry. I'm glad you came over tonight. I wish you would stay." He walked closer towards her and looked down into her eyes.

His closeness to her, the way he stared into her eyes, it was too much for her senses at that moment. She didn't want to do something that she couldn't take back. Even though she was over Steve, she reasoned she couldn't afford to get involved with a man anytime soon and especially not Vance, her boss. "I have to go." She rushed past him and out the front door to her car.

Vance stood in the doorway freezing but not able to close the door as he watched Pam run away from him yet again.

19

Vance sat on the floor in front of his unlit fireplace crying. It was the first time in a long time that he allowed his brain to travel back in time and register the details of the dreaded day that changed him forever.

He thought back to a Thanksgiving Day years ago.

He was a twenty-year-old junior in college and his brother Marcus was a twenty-four-year-old law student visiting their parents for the holiday. Wanting to spend more time with her sons, who were home from college, Mattie, their mother sent her husband to the store for more cranberry sauce to go with her dressing she had made from scratch.

Marcus Sr. loved to please his wife so he dressed for the cold Chicago winter weather and headed out of the door in search of a store that would have his wife's desire.

Marcus, Vance, and the other guys were screaming at the television screen during the football game.

"Man, that quarterback has to stay on his knees if he thinks the Broncos are going to win this." Marcus laughed as he knelt in a praying position.

"He can stay there all he wants, but the Cowboys got this in the bag. Oh, did you see that? Julian can't touch them...." Vance jumped up out of his seat pointing at the replay on the big TV screen.

"Vance, you know that prayer works." Anthony chimed in on the conversation.

"I know it does, it helped me with one false alarm pregnancy, an almost DUI (even though I wasn't technically drunk), and when I almost flunked my calculus class. All I know is that it won't help Julian now."

"Man you need to stop playing with God." Marcus admonished his brother.

"I'm not playing with Him, but Julian needs to stop playing with you making you believe that the Broncos will win."

The men jumped out of their seats cheering for the most recent play, but the game was interrupted by a news break.

'This just in, an older African-American man was found dead in the parking lot of a Jewel-Osco in Humboldt Park. He suffered gunshot wounds to his face and chest. Police are scouring the area for witnesses or evidence that will give more insight to what happened. Tune in to the nine o'clock news for more updates." The WGN broadcaster reported.

"Man that's sad to hear, but man I'm hungry. When do we eat?" The always hungry Darius asked rubbing his stomach.

"As soon as my dad gets back." Marcus promised his friends.

Vance wondered where his father was. His parents lived on the north side of Chicago in a nice neighborhood. The grocery store was nearby. His father should have been back by then seeing as though he had already been gone for nearly an hour. Vance thought to himself, "Maybe the store up the street was closed and he had to ride around out west to find an open store. Hurry home dad."

Vance left the family room and went into the kitchen.

"Ma, where is dad? He should've been back from the store by now."

Mattie smacked Vance's hand away from the caramel cake as he tried to scoop some of the icing off the top.

"You can't have any of this cake until we eat dinner and that won't happen until your father gets here. As for where he is, he should've been back by now, but you know your father, he's probably somewhere being a Good Samaritan."

"Yeah, he always has been willing to help others. No matter how much he had to do at the church, he still made sure he was at every game and academic competition for Marcus and me."

Mattie's back was turned towards Vance while she washed the pots and pans she used earlier. Vance was cutting a piece of the caramel cake sitting *out on the island. "Dad needs to hurry up and get back so that we can eat before I get in trouble for constantly doing this."*

"Doing what?" Vance ran with the stolen piece of cake in his hands past his mother as she tried to swat him with the dish towel.

"Vance, stay out of this kitchen. Mattie laughed at Vance, but her smile quickly turned into a frown wondering where her husband was.

***

Vance re-entered the family room as his brother was answering the door.

Detective Hopkins flashed his shield at Marcus and spoke. "Hello sir. May I speak with Mrs. Sutherland?"

"How may I help you detective?" Marcus stepped on the porch and closed the door behind him.

"I really need to speak with Mrs. Sutherland, sir. She is listed as the next of kin."

"Next of kin? Detective Hopkins right? If there is something you need to share with my mother then you can share it with me." Marcus leaned in and whispered something to Detective Hopkins.

"Okay. Well, I am the lead detective on the case." Detective Hopkins spoke pacing himself for the news he was about to bear.

"What case detective?"

"Earlier a man was murdered at a grocery store. We recovered his wallet in the nearby bushes. The driver's license info matched the description of the murder victim."

"Ok, and what does this have to do with my mother?"

"Marcus, the wallet belonged to your father. The picture and info on the I.D. matched Mr. Sutherland. We need your mother to come down to identify the body as her husband's."

"What?" Marcus puffed in disbelief. "Are you sure it was my father? I'm sure this is all a big misunderstanding. Maybe someone stole his wallet and the victim bears an uncanny resemblance to my father."

"We believe the deceased is Marcus Sutherland Sr., but that's why we definitely need you all to identify the body."

Marcus rubbed his face searching his thoughts for what to say next. "Let me break it to my mother and see if she even wants to go down to the morgue to handle this. Either way, I'll be down there within an hour."

"Okay, well here's my card. Call me if you need anything. I'll be at the morgue waiting on you all."

Marcus took a moment to compose himself before he reentered the house.

"Man, what's wrong with you? Who or what pissed you off?" Darius asked his lifelong friend.

"Yeah man, why you gotta look like that? As ugly as you are, you can't afford to frown." Vance chuckled trying to cheer up his brother.

Everyone in the room laughed except for Marcus.

"Lighten up man, I was joking. You're not that ugly." Vance retorted with his second attempt to cheer up his brother.

Again, everyone laughed except for Marcus.

"Who was at the door? Was that your father? Did he lose his key?" Mattie fired off the questions as she entered the family room wiping her hands dry on a dish towel.

"Ma, have a seat," Marcus spoke softly as he approached his mother and ushered her to the couch.

"What is up with you man? Why are you acting like that? It's Thanksgiving Day, your team won the game, and we are about to eat some good food as soon as daddy walks through the door. Speaking of daddy, has anyone heard from him? His phone keeps going to the voicemail when I call." Vance asked trying to distinguish his brother's solemn demeanor.

"MJ, what is going on? Why do I need to be sitting here?" Mattie asked her oldest son.

"Ma, Vance, that was a Detective Hopkins at the door." He looked to the fellas. *"You guys remember the newsbreak earlier during the game?"*

"Yeah, the one about the man murdered at Jewel?" Anthony asked concerned for his friend.

"Yeah, I saw it in the kitchen, but what does that unfortunate incident have to do with us?"

Standing over his mother but still holding her hand, Marcus tried to explain the situation, "Well they found daddy's wallet near the crime scene and they believe that the man murdered is daddy."

Mattie clutched her necklace and gasped for air as she pondered whether or not it was actually her husband.

Marcus sat down next to his mother to calm her down.

Vance jumped up out of his seat. "Come on Marcus, let's not jump to any conclusions. I know that my daddy is not dead. God wouldn't let that happen to Pastor Marcus Sutherland Sr.; a man who has devoted his entire life to doing the work of the Lord. The kindest man on earth. Not my father." Vance began pacing the floor.

"I don't want to believe it's daddy, but I've studied the protocol in school. Detectives don't go to the victim's home until they are sure of his or her identity. They solely have the family to I.D. the body for clarification, but they already know who the victim is."

"Man, how can you be so calm when it's a possibility that it's daddy in the 'city morgue'. The city morgue." Vance went into a frenzy throwing objects at the wall before he stormed out of the house.

Anthony and Darius chased after Vance as Marcus continued to console his sobbing mother.

That day, Vance gave up on believing in and serving a God who would allow such a horrendous thing to happen to one of his children, especially a loving man like his father.

20

Pam had managed to make it through another brutal Chicago winter.

She woke up that morning and instead of saying a quick prayer and rushing out of her house to prepare her classroom for the day she decided to spend some quiet time with God on the balcony at the back of her house.

It wasn't quite as warm as she would have preferred it to be for a spring morning, but she couldn't ignore the beautiful array of flowers that bloomed in the community garden behind her condo building.

The sight was breathtaking to Pam. She stood leaning against the banister sipping on Chai tea.

God I thank You for everything that You've done for me and all that You plan to do. I thank You for the sisterhood that I have with Kim, Renee, and Monica. I thank You for being able to depend on them as my earthly sources of inspiration and listening ears. Thank You that they have a relationship with You and tell me what I need to hear from You even when I ignore You speaking directly to me.

She took a deep breath before continuing. *I thank You for forgiving me of my affair with Steve. I thank You so much God for showing me how to forgive myself that I am able to enjoy this moment with You right now, my life without condemning myself. I will wait on You to bless me with the man that is for me and led by You. I won't allow moments of loneliness to make me feel as if I have to settle for less than Your best for me. God I thank You for the beauty that You've allowed Sharday to see in herself and the friendships that she has gained with her classmates.*

Pam smiled and wiped a tear.

I thank you for Asia's turnaround. I don't know what the situation is between her parents right now, but no matter what it is, thank You God that she feels Your love. Thank You God for giving me a heart for young girls and as I do my first official mentoring session with them today, I pray that You bless it. In Jesus' name, Amen.

Pam had finished drinking her tea. She turned on her heels ready to head back into her house, but she felt led to say something else to God. *Okay God, You know my heart, my thoughts, my everything. Speaking of my heart, please change it where my mother is concerned. I know I've been avoiding her and when I do speak to her I'm short with her. My avoidance of her has negatively impacted my relationship with my dad because I've been avoiding him to avoid her as well. I know that I am not supposed to harbor ill feelings for anyone, especially not my mother, so fix it Lord. Change her heart so that whenever we do speak again there can be a different ending or a new beginning to our story.* She took a deep breath before speaking again. A frown formed on her face. *God I don't understand why my attraction to Vance has not gone away. No matter how much I've prayed to You for You to take it away, busied myself with other things to do, I think about him often, and when I see him, well You know the butterflies that form in my stomach. The visions of walking down the aisle to him. How chocolate our kids will be.* She laughed out loud. *Well God, He's been so formal with me, since that night I left his house after the argument we had. He's my boss, and since he doesn't believe in You, he should be out of the question for me, so can You please share that with my heart? It would be greatly appreciated if You would work this miracle for me. Thanks.* Pam walked away from her prayer hopeful that God would grant her request.

***

Pam made it early to school as usual.

There were only two other cars there besides hers, Curtis, the engineer, and Vance's.

She drudged up the stairs headed to the main office knowing the likelihood of seeing Vance was high. She wasn't ready for her stomach to perform its daily somersaults whenever she saw him or he was near to her so she hoped that he wouldn't be visible in the office.

Curtis the engineer was busy mopping the hallway floors when she entered the main office to clock in and Vance's intoxicating cologne filled her nostrils. Her heart jumped looking at the broadness of his back through his suit coat. *Okay God, I see You didn't get the memo yet, but can You please take my attraction away for this man ASAP. I'm begging you please.*

Pam swiped her I.D. card through the machine and laughed at herself talking to God as if He were some type of genie.

Vance looked up from his desk to see Pam. He looked back down at the files on his desk before he spoke to her. "Good morning Ms. Robinson."

"Uh, hi V…uh Mr. Sutherland."

Not looking at her, he continued to speak. "I know your mentoring program starts after school today, so email me if you need anything other than what's already been provided."

"Okay." She looked at him hoping he would look up at her, but he never did.

She rounded the countertop, grabbed the mail from her mailbox, and left the main office.

She had snacks and other items in her hand for her session after school so Curtis helped her up the stairs with all of her bags. She was sad remembering that was something Vance would have eagerly done for her months before.

Because Pam loved what she did, the school day flew by as usual for her, in fact, she wish she had more time to spend with her students each day. But on this day she was looking forward to what she would be doing after school with the girls.

After many of the teacher's in the upper grades saw how Pam's intervention with Asia and Sharday's situation changed them for the better, they referred a few of their female students to her.

Each of the referred girls took a liking to Pam immediately. She had so many one on one consultations with the girls daily that she figured it would be feasible for her to create a more structured program for the girls where she could mentor them and better yet, they would be able to mentor each other and provide support and positive intervention for one another as they dealt with the day to day woes of being adolescent and pre-teenage girls.

All of the girls she invited to the program were now in her room.

"Hello ladies."

"Hi, Ms. Robinson." They all smiled at her as they spoke collectively.

They each took a seat in the circle of chairs Pam had created in the middle of the room.

She came and stood in the middle of it and rotated as she spoke. "Per your invitations, you all know why we're here, to support one another, to encourage one another. I know you may be thinking like, 'how can she or she or she or she help me with what I go through and they're my age?' Well, I'll tell you that it's possible to learn something from people your age. I happen to have three of the best friends a woman could ask for."

"Ms. Robinson has BFF's." One girl called out causing the others to laugh.

"Do y'all talk on Snapchat and Instagram to each other?" Another girl called out and some girls joined her in laughing.

Pam smiled. "No, when we need to talk to each other we either call, text, or show up at one another's houses. Anway, I have the pleasure of talking to many of you all daily, if not weekly. It isn't always bad, but to help you all grow even more into the beautiful young ladies I know you can be, we will meet once a week to discuss things. You'll also have a mentoring partner that you'll be responsible for keeping up with."

A few of the girls turned their noses up.

"Why the frowns ladies?"

"Becuz, I don't want er'body up in my bizness like that." One of the girls smacked her lips after she spoke.

"True." A few more girls affirmed the statement.

"If we create a safe and trusting environment as I plan to-"

There was a knock at the door.

Pam turned her head to see who it could be interrupting her session at such a key moment in the discussion.

It was Vance.

She rubbed her hair making sure it was in place, smoothed out her dress, and headed to the door. "Give me a second ladies, why don't you all come up with a name for the group while I speak with Mr. Sutherland."

The classroom immediately bubbled over with the noise of the girls trying to figure out what the mentoring group's name would be.

"Yes, Mr. Sutherland." Pam looked into his eyes. She didn't see that same admiration he used to have for her but rather a poised air of concern for her.

"Ms. Robinson, your dad called up to the school."

Pam's eyebrows furrowed. "Hunh, why'd he call the school? He has my number."

"He said he couldn't reach you." Vance stood with his hands crossed in front of him.

"Oh that's right, I never turned my phone back on when school let out. Okay, thanks for letting me know. I'll call him when I get done with the girls." The eerie tension between her and Vance was too much for her to handle at that moment. Pam turned to walk back in the classroom, but Vance pulled her arm to keep her in place.

She looked down at his hand on her arm. There was something in the way he held her arm. She slowly allowed her eyes to travel back up to his.

"Ms. Robinson, Pam." Pure compassion oozed from every being of his body. "It's your mom."

"What about her?" Pam folded her arms at her chest pulling away from Vance.

Vance looked at her for a moment. After she left his house the day he didn't make it to work, he decided it was best not to try and win her over anymore. Although he still very much cared for her, he hated rejection just as much as the next person. His feelings for her didn't go away but he felt the need to pull back from her, grant her request of keeping things formal between them. He wished his heart would cooperate with his thinking.

"What about her?" Pam screamed but looked in the room to make sure the girls didn't hear her outburst.

The girls didn't hear Pam because they were still busy deciding what their name would be and who would be the leaders of the group.

Vance spoke demanding her attention again. "Your dad said she fell earlier and hit her head."

"Okay. Once I wrap things up with the girls, I'll head over to the house to see her." Pam turned to head back in the classroom again.

Vance stopped her in her tracks yet again. "No, you don't understand, hitting her head caused her to have a seizure. It wouldn't stop. They rushed her to the hospital and now she's in surgery to relieve the pressure of the swelling and the hemorrhaging." Vance reached out to keep Pam from falling as he saw her grow faint.

Rather than run from him that time as she often did, she allowed her body to rest against his as she tried to make sense of what he said.

He held her close to him. He knew it was his duty to share that information with her since he took the call. He couldn't help but to enjoy her closeness to him, even though the reason why she was so close to him wasn't in her favor. He inhaled the sweet scent of her hair and his heart ached. He could never gather why he cared for her the way he did knowing the divide between them. "How about you go to the restroom and compose yourself while I go in and dismiss the girls."

"Thanks." Pam wiped tears from her face on her way to the bathroom.

Vance went into the classroom and made up an excuse as to why the girls wouldn't see Pam for the rest of the meeting. He dismissed them from the session and walked them outside.

By the time he made it back in Pam stood in the office alone crying silent tears and shaking as she tried to steady her hand to swipe out. "Ms. Robinson, are you okay to drive right now?" He walked over to her.

Pam was oblivious to Vance as she swiped out and headed down the stairs thinking of what condition her mother was in.

Her father and her brothers were calling her phone often, but she wasn't ready to talk to them. She feared what they might say to her.

Vance caught up with her in the parking lot. She stood at the driver's side door of Curtis the engineer's car. "Ms. Robinson, come on."

"What?" She looked up to recognize Vance as the one leading her away from the car.

"What are you doing? I have to go see my ma-ma-mom." Pam stuttered the last of her statement.

He looked at her. "Pam, that wasn't your car. You're in no shape to drive right now. I'll take you." Vance led her to the passenger side of his car. He grabbed the bags from her hand and placed them on the backseat. He opened the door and helped her up to be seated. He had to fasten her seatbelt for her because she was too distraught to do it herself.

Vance got in the driver's seat, started up the car, and dialed the school phone. "Hello, yes Mrs. Jackson, I have something urgent to handle. I won't be back in the building. Can you please lock up my office and tell Curtis you'll be staying with him tonight to secure the building?...Okay, thanks." Vance ended his call with the assistant principal.

He looked over at Pam. Tears streamed from her eyes and she seemed to hold her breath for moments at a time before she exhaled then held it again. Her stare was focused ahead of her but not on any particular thing.

Fortunately, her father had given him the name of the hospital and Vance wouldn't have to rely on Pam to tell her where to take her.

He knew how close she was with Ms. Williams, Kim, and he thought to call her back up to the school to be with Pam, but his heart wouldn't let him. He couldn't explain what kept him liking Pam. All he knew was that he did and he wanted to be there to support her with whatever was going on with her mother, although he wouldn't show her he was still interested in her.

Vance let the silence in the car engulf them as he drove to the hospital.

He made it there in record time, valet parked, and escorted Pam into the lobby area of the hospital. Knowing what wing and room of the hospital her mother was in Vance held Pam's arm as he was walking past a receptionist at the front desk.

"Excuse me sir, you have to have a pass to go past this point."

"I'm sorry." Vance backed up still holding Pam's arm.

She wasn't even aware of her surroundings.

Vance spoke to the older woman. "She's here to see her mother who is still in surgery, but her father told me that he and his sons are waiting in the post-op waiting area."

She looked at Vance. "Well only immediate family is allowed up in that area, but it seems as if she won't be able to make it up there on her own, so I'll allow you to go up too." She handed Vance the two visiting passes and winked at him. "Go past the gift shop there and take that elevator to the seventh floor. When you get off, go to your right, press the button and go through the double doors. The nurse up there will let you walk past since I'm calling her now to let her know I'm letting you up there as well."

"Thank you." Vance nodded his head.

Pam seemed to be coming out her catatonic state the longer they walked down the hall after passing through the double doors.

She tried to speak to Vance but her mouth was so dry and her tears wouldn't stop flowing. She loosened her elbow with his, entwined her fingers with his and squeezed his hand.

He stopped their stride to look her in the eyes. "Pam, it's going to be okay." He hoped he sounded convincing to her seeing as though he didn't believe what he was saying himself, but he knew she was a believer. He thought he should say something to try and comfort her.

She looked in his eyes for hope and when she couldn't find it, she pulled away from him.

"Just go."

"No, I want to make sure that you'll be okay."

"Okay? My mother could be dead and you think I'll be okay." Pam stared into his eyes.

"I've been where you are now, no matter the outcome you'll cope with it in time."

"What do you mean you've been where I've been?"

Vance put his head down. He didn't want to share that painful part of his past even with Pam.

"Like I thought, you don't know what I'm going through. My mother and I have been at odds for years. I've barely spoken to her in months, so for me to find out that she's having major surgery right now and may not come out of it tears me apart. You don't know what I'm going through." Pam screamed oblivious to where she was at the moment.

Her father heard her from in the waiting room and rushed to her to see what had her so upset.

"Pam, sweetie, is everything okay?"

She looked to her right and saw her father. She threw herself in his arms and wept.

"It'll be okay, we know the effectual fervent prayers of the righteous availeth much." Melvin rubbed her back. He looked up at Vance. "Oh you must be Mr. Sutherland?"

"Yes sir, I am."

Pam's dad extended his hand and firmly shook Vance's.

"Thank you for getting her here safely. Her brothers were in no condition to drive to get her and I won't leave my wife's side until I see her beautiful smile again and hear her voice." Melvin smiled as a tear escaped his eye.

Vance smiled hearing the warmth in Melvin's voice talking about his wife. His heart ached remembering how he used to hear his dad talk about his mom with such tenderness.

"Is everything okay? I heard her screaming and I came to see what was wrong." Melvin asked.

Vance shrugged his shoulders.

"If this were a more joyous occasion, I would offer you to stay with us and enjoy your company, but right now, I can't say we would be any fun to you." Melvin pulled Pam closer to him as her sobs grew louder.

"It's okay, sir. I know you need time to be with your family. When Pam feels better, tell her I'll make sure we have a sub in her room for her tomorrow and tell her to call to the school and let us know if she needs more days off after tomorrow." Vance gave Melvin a half smirk.

"Thank you, Mr. Sutherland." Melvin reached out to shake Vance's hand again. "Thank you for all you've done."

"My pleasure, sir." Vance did a roundabout and headed back to the elevators bewildered.

***

"Mr. Robinson." The surgeon came from the operating room calling out to Melvin.

Melvin rushed to the surgeon.

Pam and her brothers went and planked their father.

"Sir, the surgery was successful in alleviating the pressure on her brain and we managed to stop the bleeding. We won't know the effects of the fall and the surgery until after the swelling goes down and she's had some time to recover." The surgeon looked at the sadness in each of their eyes. "I wish there was more that I could tell you, but I can't at this point. You all will be able to stop in and see her in about an hour after they transfer her over to the ICU." The surgeon nodded his head with an "I'm sorry" look on his face and headed back into the O.R.

Pam leaned in closer to her dad. He draped his arm around her as she wept.

***

Her mother's surgery happened on a Tuesday and it was now Saturday morning and Pam sat in the chair next to her bed side.

She hadn't left the hospital despite her brothers and her father pleading with her to go home, eat, shower, and return once she had gotten some rest.

She didn't understand how after she had rid herself of the guilt of her affair with Steve that she now still had to deal with her mother's stay in the hospital. The guilt of barely speaking to her mother recently because she was so tired of her mother's judgmental ways was gnawing at her.

She thought that she would have the chance to reconcile her relationship with her mother in time, but the fall and emergency surgery happened. She didn't know what she would do with herself if her mother never woke up. She smiled a little looking out at the trees lining the parking lot. She thought back to how supportive the sisterhood had been since her mom's surgery. At least one of them stopped by daily to check on her and get an update on her mom.

If they weren't all there for them to pray together for her mother's total healing, then they would do a conference call prayer.

Pam was holding her mom's hand when she felt a tug on her arm. She looked over at her mom and Eilene's eyes were fluttering. She panicked not knowing if Eilene was having another seizure or not. She jumped from her seat to grab the button to call for a nurse but the faint sound of her mother's voice and a tighter squeeze of her hand stopped her.

"Pam?" Eilene whispered with her eyes closed.

Pam wiped the tears from her eyes trying not to worry her mother as she readied herself to speak. "Yes ma'am." Pam leaned in closer to her mother and kissed her cheeks.

Still whispering, Eilene spoke. "Why haven't you gone home yet and showered? You stink and I'm certain you look a mess." Eilene tried to laugh but chocked on her breaths.

"Oh mom, don't try to talk." Pam pulled back from her mom and tried to press the button for an attendant again but Eilene stopped her with a tight squeeze on Pam's hand. Pam smiled through her tears. On one hand, she was happy that her mother was now awake with what seemed like no memory problems, but then again she was still as judgmental as ever talking about her hygiene or that she probably looked bad when she chose to stay by her side while she was in the hospital. *Lord help me to love her and respect her no matter what.*

"Pam?" Eilene said low.

"Yes ma'am." Pam looked up to see her mother trying to sit up more than the bed was allowing her to. She rushed back to her side. "Mom, you have to take it easy. Do you know what happened to you?"

"Yes I do." Eilene's voice was a little bit stronger now and Pam didn't have to lean in so close to hear her. "I fell and hit my head and now, I'm here in what looks to be a hospital room." Eilene scanned the room. "All of this for a little fall?" She looked at all of the tubes hooked up to her.

Pam wiped more tears from her eyes and cleared her throat before she spoke again. "Mom, you didn't just fall and hit your head and that was it. When you fell and hit your head, it triggered a seizure. You had a lot of cranial bleeding, no oxygen was getting to your brain, so they had to do emergency surgery to relieve the pressure."

Eilene's face saddened. "So what is today?"

"Today is Saturday, mom."

"I fell Tuesday, right?"

"Yes ma'am."

"So I've been out of it since Tuesday?" Eilene choked on her tears.

Pam grabbed the cup of water.

"I'm okay. I don't need water now. So where is your father? Your brothers?"

"Dad and Jr. are in the waiting room. Eric is at work right now, but he's been coming up here everyday during his lunch hour. They get upset with me because only one of us can be in here at a time with you and I refuse to leave your side."

"Mmph. I would think you would want to be as far away from me as possible." Tears trickled down Eilene's pale face.

"Why would you say that mom?" Pam drew even closer to her mother.

"Because, you don't seem to like me." She turned her head away from Pam. "You stay away from me as long as you possibly can, if and when you do come over it's to see your father and then I don't hear from you for weeks later."

"That's because…" Pam didn't know if it was the time to share how she felt about her mother with her. She was worried the conversation would cause her mother unnecessary stress at that time.

"Because what?" Eilene turned to look at Pam. With a squeeze of her hand, she pushed Pam to speak.

Pam was speechless. For the first time in a long time, Pam saw a genuine look of concern rather than contempt in her mother's eyes.

"Because, you're always so judgmental of me. I never seem to do anything right in your eyes." Pam wiped her face. "No matter how many things I accomplish in life, you seem to shine the light on the wrong things I've done."

"But-"

"No mom, I'm sorry, I don't mean to cut you off and I certainly don't want to upset you, but I need to say this while I have the strength to."

Eilene nodded her head with her eyes closed and Pam continued.

Pam took a deep breath. "I would love to have the kind of relationship with you that Kim and Renee have with their mother, but I don't." Tears flowed from Pam's eyes. "I know I haven't done everything the exact way you've wanted me to, but it's my life mom. It's my life. You have to let me live it and love me through my mistakes. Not continue to hold them against me."

Eilene tried to speak but Pam cut her off again. "No, please, let me finish, you need to save your strength anyway." Pam softened her stare at her mother and then continued speaking, "it was this and that when I was younger. Why'd I go into teaching instead of something that would make me more money? Why wasn't I married with kids by twenty-five? And then when I met the man I thought I would marry only to find out he was already married, you dogged me out even more. You alienated me, mom."

"I didn't alienate you." Eilene said as strong as she could.

"You did." Pam sighed. "I wanted nothing more than to come running to you the night that I found out he was married and you would hold me while I cried, but I couldn't come to you." Pam folded her arms at her chest. "I guess I let it slip out to you hoping that you would somehow comfort me, but you berated me every chance you could. Don't you think I was condemning myself enough for the both of us?"

Pam wanted to go on, but Eilene mustered up as much strength as she could to interrupt Pam. "Pamela Shanice Robinson, shut up and let me talk." Eilene fell back on her pillow and closed her eyes taking deep breaths allowing her blood pressure to lower before she spoke again.

Pam rushed to her side and squeezed her hand. "Oh momma, I'm sorry, I shouldn't have brought this stuff up now, not here. Let's save it until after you've fully recovered."

Pam turned to walk away, but Eilene tightened her grip on Pam's hand again.

The beeping on the monitor sped up.

Pam looked back at Eilene before Eilene slowly opened her eyes.

Eilene looked up at Pam with tears in her eyes. "Baby, you just don't know a mother's love yet. When you have children, you have hopes and dreams for them. Sometimes, for some of us, when we don't see those dreams become a reality we get upset and say things we shouldn't." Eilene turned away from Pam for a minute. She laughed. She then turned back towards Pam and her stare into Pam's eyes tempered even more. "I admit that my words have been harsh towards you and I may not have acted towards you the way you've wanted me to, but it's tearing me up right now knowing that you think that I didn't or don't love you. When I found out about you sleeping with a married man, my heart hurt as a wife and as your mother. The wife in me was angry for you not being more conscious, more prayerful into what kind of man he was before you gave yourself to him, and then to stay with him after you found out he was married. That hurt me as a wife." The monitors beeped faster.

"Ma this is upsetting you, your blood pressure is rising. Let's save this conversation until you've fully recovered."

"A little elevated blood pressure never hurt anyone." Eilene laughed.

"Mom."

"I'm serious, I know one would think that with what happened to me and so soon after it that I should still be out of it and so weak, but since my God is in the healing business, I'm fine."

Pam and Eilene smiled at each other.

"Pam, I love you sweetie. It's never been my intention to hurt you with what I say, it's that as a mother I expected so much out of you, my only girl, my baby girl, my beautiful, brilliant baby girl who I thought I raised to be confident but to find out that you were outside of the will of God with your sex life and sleeping with a married man," Eilene shed more tears. She paused to catch her breath before she continued to speak. "It didn't make me look at you as a failure, but that I failed you in raising you not to settle for less than God's best for you."

"Mom, I don't know what to say."

"Well you've been sharing your heart all of this time, don't stop now."

They both laughed.

"It's that, forgive me for sounding disrespectful for what I'm about to say."

Eilene raised one eyebrow as she stared at Pam.

Pam stepped back from Eilene.

"You seem to contradict yourself."

"Oh really?"

The lilt in Eilene's voice made Pam stepped back even more. "Yes ma'am. On one hand you were judging yourself for my behavior feeling that you somehow failed me because I wasn't waiting for God's best for me but instead being with a married man, which by the way, I didn't know that when he and I first started dating."

Eilene cut Pam off as she sat up some. "But you were having sex with him and y'all weren't married, right?"

"Yes ma'am."

"And did you end your affair with him the minute you found out he was married?"

"No ma'am." Pam averted eye contact with her mother.

Eilene rested her head back on her pillow and folded her arms across her chest. She smirked.

"I admit that I'm wrong for all of that. I carried the guilt of my sins for over the past year. I'm finally free from condemning myself and I won't let you condemn me any longer for it either." Pam looked her mother in the eyes. She stepped back even further from her bed side.

Eilene sat up some and turned her head towards Pam. Her eyebrows furrowed.

"I won't let you condemn me any more, mom."

Eilene stared Pam down as best as she could.

Pam stuttered. "God has forgiven me, so you better get over it. And, and, if you don't, then you'll have to take that up with God." She stepped back even further until she could sit on the window ledge in the room. She was definitely out of Eilene's reach. She felt safe there.

Eilene smirked at Pam. "Take it up with God hunh?"

"Yes ma'am. You say you felt like you failed to raise me with confidence to wait on God's best for my love life, but did you ever stop and ask yourself if you were treating me the way God wanted you to treat me, your daughter?"

Eilene rested her head on the pillow again and turned her head away from Pam.

"I guess not. The same Bible that tells children to honor their mother and father that they may have long days on the earth is the same Bible that tells parents that their children are a gift from God. We don't do our gifts any kind of way when we get them, right? We appreciate them and operate them the way they were designed." Pam felt the confidence to go on. "Even before my affair with this guy, you were hard on me, wishing I would've become something that made more money than a teacher. When I was in high school, you complained about all the time I was spending over Kim and Renee's house. You said I should've been focusing more on my studies to become a doctor or lawyer, but you never understood that I always wanted to be over there because of the love their mother showed them. She treated me as if I was hers too. There was always such a warmth there. The only time I felt that way here was when I was in daddy's arms." Pam wiped at the streams of tears that flowed from her eyes.

Eilene kept her head turned away from Pam.

The beeping of the monitors grew louder and the distance between the beeps shortened.

Pam rushed to her mom's bedside. "Mom?"

She leaned over Eilene to see her eyes roll to the back of her head as her body convulsed violently.

"Somebody help. Help! She's seizing again."

21

"Praise the Lord saints. I said, praise the Lord saints." The elderly deacon tried to rile the congregation up before his prayer. He asked everyone to bow their heads as he gathered himself on one knee.

The youthful pastor of the church smiled at the deacon on bended knee remembering how many times he had told the deacon it wasn't necessary for him to pray like that. He was ushering the Baptist congregation into the understanding that God looks at the heart more so than one's physical posture in prayer. Ten minutes into the prayer, Pastor Riley let out a small chuckle looking at the faces of the youth in the congregation. Their eyes rolled, lips smacked, necks were cocked to the side, and unfortunately, many of them seemed to be glued to whatever had their attention on their cell phones. Sadly enough, there were a few adults exhibiting the same behavior.

Pastor Riley's focus zoomed in on Vance. Vance sat at the back of the church in a posture that seemed as if he were being held there at gunpoint.

Upon taking over as the head pastor sometime after Pastor Sutherland's death, Pastor Riley was informed of how one brother continued on in the ministry while one completely lost his faith in God.

He knew who was who because Marcus Sutherland Jr. attended church every Wednesday and Sundays. Marcus was involved in the youth and men's ministry, while this was the first time he had saw Vance face to face. He only recognized him because of the pictures Vance's mother showed him of her son, the elementary school principal. Pastor Riley said a prayer to himself asking God to speak through him directly to Vance during the service.

He was glad the deacon had finally ended his prayer. The praise and worship team was gearing up to sing songs to the Lord. He tried to mix the old with the new in terms of how he ran the service. He allowed the deacons to do devotion but knew it was vital for the praise and worship team to set the atmosphere before he delivered his message. He wanted the hearts and ears of the congregation to be open to the voice of God.

The leader of the praise and worship team started singing.

Vance jumped up and walked out the door. He made it all the way down the front steps and was headed to the parking lot when Marcus caught up with him.

"Vance. Where are you going man? Please, don't leave."

Vance turned around to face Marcus. "I only agreed to come here because of mom. You're my brother and I love you, but I could care less what you think about how I live my life. I wanted to put a smile on her face today."

"And do you think she will be smiling when she stands up as they are honoring dad for what he did for this church, this community, and you're nowhere to be seen?"

"I can't take the hypocrisy." Vance threw his hands in the air as if he were praising God. "Praise the Lord Saints! Puh-raise the Lord!" He shuffled his feet and bucked his head as if he were full of the Holy Ghost and shouting.

Marcus stood there staring at his younger brother. "Come on man, stop playing with God."

Vance stopped "shouting" but broke out in an uproarious laughter. "You're telling me stop playing with God? Well do you tell any of them in there that were at the club last night, in bed with someone their not married to, or someone else's husband or wife to stop playing with God? Better yet, do you tell God to stop playing with humanity making them think that He's everywhere, that He knows everything, that He cares so much about us, but He couldn't even keep our daddy from being shot and killed? And in the same neighborhood he spent so much time helping out. I bet you don't do that." Vance walked closer to Marcus and pointed his finger in his face. "I hate this neighborhood, I hate this church. And I hate your God."

"But do you love your mother?"

"Man, you know I do."

"I'mma keep praying for you, but I won't carry the burden any longer of trying to get you back on track with God. It's between you and Him now, like it's always been."

"He and I have nothing to talk about because he doesn't exist." Vance threw his hands up in the air through his exasperated breath.

Marcus stepped back in case God struck his brother down at that moment. He inwardly laughed at himself for the thought, but he kept his distance from Vance. "So at least do this for mom then."

Vance huffed. "Of course I'll do it for her, but I won't sit in there during the singing and the sermon. Text me right before they are ready to do the part where they'll honor dad and expect us to be up there with mom."

"Nope."

"Come on man, why not?"

"Because I won't. If you wanna know your cue when to go up there, then you better be in there yourself." Marcus patted Vance on the arm and walked back in the church. He hoped praise and worship wasn't done.

Vance stood alone on the sidewalk contemplating if he should sit in his car and chance going back in when he thought it would be time for him to go stand next to his mother for his father's tribute. He didn't want to see the sadness on her face if he was nowhere to be found when they honored his dad, so he figured he would try and stomach another hour or so of what he thought was pure buffoonery going on in the church. He stood outside for a bit longer though. When he went back in he was glad to see that the singing portion of service was over but hated that he would have to sit through the sermon.

He stared at the young looking pastor. *Who is this guy anyway? He could never compare to my father. My father was tall with broad shoulders, piercing almost black eyes. My dad was distinguished, and a voice that could penetrate the core of your soul with his words.* Vance looked at the pastor longer, ignoring what was being said. *He or no one else could ever take my father's place as the leader of this church.*

Vance glanced over at the teenage boy next to him looking at half-naked Instagram models. He smiled seeing the boy ignoring the sermon like he was. He didn't have an Instagram account to fixate on the women on there like the boy next to him, instead he let his mind drift to thoughts of Pam. He wondered how she and her mother were doing. He hoped thinking of Pam would overshadow the memories he was having of his dad and his life before his father was killed.

Pastor Riley spoke drowning out Vance's thoughts of Pam. "It is imperative that we not blame God for what does and what doesn't happen in our lives."

Now he's saying something I agree with. We can't rely on God because we in and of ourselves control what does or doesn't happen to us. We are the highest forms of ourselves.

"If we would be totally honest with ourselves, a lot of things that happen in our lives is because of our own actions." Pastor Riley said.

This man knows what he's talking about. Vance sat up to listen to Pastor Riley. *These sheep don't even know this man ain't leading them to God but to themselves. Yes, the way it should be.*

"I know somebody out there is thinking and saying to themselves, 'Pastor, well what about death, cancer, blindness, rape, all of that bad stuff that people don't bring on themselves?"

It seemed as if the entire church was on the edge of their seats listening for his response.

"Well, I don't profess to know everything, but some scriptures come to mind that comfort me when trying to make sense of the violence and decay that happens in the world. For one, the Bible clearly states in Ecclesiastes 3 that there is a time and a season for everything. A time to mourn, a time to die. Yes, I know we would love to be immortal, but we can thank or hold a grudge with Adam and Eve for changing that for us."

The congregation laughed.

"But seriously, we know that after that day some things were promised to mankind as a result for stepping outside of the will of God. Satan took dominion over the earth that day as a result of the fall, but God had a plan to make sure that we would be restored back to our rightful places as rulers and citizens in the kingdom of God."

What is wrong with him? Lying to these people. He lost me again.

"God sent His Son to live and die for us to give us dominion back over the earth. But guess what?"

"What Pastor?" A mother of five children jumped up shouting.

"We act like we don't believe we have dominion over this earth and everything in it. Until we unite as the body of Christ and take our place in the earth realm, we can expect much more decay to take place."

Vance smacked his lips.

"We wonder why God didn't save our loved one who was killed due to the violence of these Chicago streets," Pastor Riley paused. "I imagine this would shake a person to their core if it were someone who they truly loved and valued, but you must take comfort in knowing that if they had a relationship with God they are with Him now. The question is, with the way you are living now, will you see that loved one again in eternity?"

Vance tried to get up from his seat to leave out, but it seemed as if he weren't allowed to get up by some force outside of himself.

"We all have to leave this earth one day, whether it be before or during the rapture, we just don't know the when and the how. When someone's 'how' to the ending of their life doesn't suit you, that doesn't mean you get mad at God and turn your back on Him. That's when you draw closer to Him all the more. If you really did read the word and believe in it, you would know that only good things come from God."

"Amen pastor." Someone shouted.

"He wishes above all that you would be in good health and prosper. It is the devil that comes to kill, steal, and destroy. Whether that be the very breath they breathe, their good health, their financial fortune, or whatever it may be. In the case of death, sickness and other calamities, you're assigning the cause of that thing to the wrong person. It's not God who takes in those cases, it's the devil."

"You better tell it like it is." A woman jumped to her feet.

"Yes the Lord allows bad things to happen because He knows that He can help you get through whatever you face in life if you trust in Him with your pain, shame, or whatever it may be. Trust me, a man standing here that has seen some horrible things in my lifetime," Pastor Riley paused wondering if he should tell his testimony, but he knew it had to be told for someone else's deliverance that day. "I've never shared this with any of you all since I've been here, but I feel that if I do now, it might bless someone today."

He came out from behind the pulpit and stepped down to be level with the rest of the congregation. "At the age of thirteen I witnessed my father murder my mother and seven-year-old sister."

The congregation gasped.

"My Lord." A mother in the corner shouted in her raspy voice.

Pastor Riley figured he might as well finish telling them the whole story. "You see, my father seemed to love me and my sister but was nasty and abusive to my mother. He was always drunk and I thought he may have been doing drugs as well."

He was now in the center aisle holding on to the back of the first pew. "The day it happened, I sat in the hallway dribbling my basketball trying to drown out the sounds of my mother and father arguing. I knew it would end with her face bruised or limbs broken as they had been so many times before. I planned to go in after her last scream and hold ice to her face knowing she would still try and get me to see the good in my daddy. Well, as I sat in that hallway listening to the dribbling of the ball, I heard my sister's screams mixed in with my mother's."

He took steps to the second pew and then held on to the back of it.

"I had always told her to stay in her room when our parents argued. I wanted to take her outside that day when the beating started, but my daddy threatened to beat me if either one of us left the house." Pastor Riley shook his head. "Usually I took the beatings, but since I hadn't fully recovered from the last one and I still had a cast on my wrist, I wasn't in the mood to be such a strong big brother that day." He shook his head. "I sat in the hallway dribbling the ball with the door cracked so my dad would know I wasn't completely gone. You see, I let my sister have the room we shared to herself to create the magical kingdom she wanted for her and her dolls. I was dribbling what I hoped would be my troubles away when a pop came from in the house that didn't sound like the ball hitting the floor. Living in the projects, I knew what gunshots sounded like, I just had never heard them coming from inside my house. 'Daddy no,' I heard my little sister scream. I jumped up to see what was going on, but before I could get through the door, I heard another pop. I raced faster to the kitchen, and by the time I made it there I heard the last pop and saw the effects of it."

Pastor Riley was now at the third pew gripping the back of it tightly. He let his head fall into his chest as recounted his last memory of his mother and sister. He lifted his head again and spoke into the microphone so that the entire congregation could hear him. "My dad had killed my mother, accidentally shot my sister panicking from her screams, and then shot himself in the head realizing he had killed his little girl. I saw him take his own life. I was speechless as I looked down at the kitchen floor to see my mother's, my sister's, and my father's blood fusing together in one big puddle on the floor."

Many of the members in the church were in tears.

The boy next to Vance was stiff with shock. His phone had fallen from his hand to the floor.

Pastor Riley spoke as he slowly walked the center aisle towards the back of the church. "You see church, I could've easily cursed God that day, but I didn't. He wouldn't let me and I thank Him for it."

Hallelujahs were echoed throughout the church.

"Through all the beatings and mistreatment, my mother went to every service at the church praying and listening to the word of God. She prayed that

God would change my daddy's heart towards her. She didn't want to break her marriage vows. You say God didn't answer her prayers, well I look at it kind of differently. She didn't suffer anymore after that day. Would I love to see her again? Yes. Would I love to see the kind of woman my little sister would've grown up to be? Yes." Pastor Riley smiled wiping a tear from his eye. "I would even love to see my father now. I believe he would be different seeing the man I grew up to be. Through it all, I chose to trust God. We can question Him all we want about why He lets this and that happen in our lives and to the people we love, but if He doesn't answer you the way you want him to, what will you do then? I'll tell you what you can do, trust that all things work together for those who love God and our called according to His purpose. I'll tell you another thing, every single human on this earth has been called by God for a specific thing, the issue is whether or not you'll accept the call."

"Now out of all I said, someone still may be doubting that God is real because of what He *let* happen to me, remember He didn't cause it He just let it happen." Pastor Riley was at Vance's row now. He stared him right in the eyes as he spoke. "But I'll ask you this, how is your life going without God?"

He turned and walked back up to the pulpit. He looked at various members of the congregation. "It's one thing to never have had a relationship with God at all, because quite frankly, that person doesn't know what exactly is missing in their life. These people search everywhere in life for something to satiate that thirst, but they never will fill it unless they come to know God in an intimate way. But, but," he perked up, "for those of you who are backslidden, that have turned away from the faith because of what you think God did to you or didn't for you, you've been out there looking and searching to fill that void that only God can fill. Only Jehovah Shalom, the God of peace, can do it. Yes, you've been running from God, but now it's time to run to God." Pastor Riley paused for a second and closed his eyes.

He silently said thanks to God for the revelation he had received then he proceeded to speak. "I believe there is someone in here, some young person that is witnessing your mother being abused by a man. Instead of running to God like I did and letting him comfort you, you're running away from God and getting yourself into trouble that could be fatal for you if you don't change your ways and thinking."

"Mmh hmm." The boy's mom sitting next to the boy on Vance's left chimed in. "If you don't stop running them streets, you probably will get locked up for good." The woman saidthrough her swollen lips and nodded her head as her over-sized shades shielded her eyes.

The boy spoke with venom dripping from his lips. "Well them streets better than being in that house watching Roy use you as his punching bag and trick you out to all of his friends."

She punched him in his arm as inconspicuously as she could. "Watch how you talk to me and lower your voice before someone else hears you. Nobody needs to know what goes on in our house." She leaned in whispering to him.

"Haaa. You think these church folks don't already know? You think all them niggas you tricking off with ain't telling everybody how many ways they've had you?" The boy continued looking down at his phone.

The woman slapped him. "Shut up you hear me. Shut up." Tears rolled from under her shades as she tried to compose herself while much of the congregation stared at them.

He put his baseball cap on his head backward, stood up holding his pants to keep them from falling, although he wore a belt, and shuffled past Vance and out the door.

Pastor Riley cleared his throat drawing the congregation's attention back to him. "There's somebody else in here that has turned their back to God because of what you feel He *did* because, and this is me speaking, He allowed it to happen. He knew that if you trusted Him through the pain you would come out victorious. I know it was your mother or father who was taken away from you." He locked eyes with Vance. "Let God off the hook for it."

Vance jumped up and walked out of the church again.

Pastor Riley was pissing him off.

Vance stepped off the last step of the front of the church to find the boy who sat next to him during the service off to the side smoking a cigarette.

"I thought you would've left after what happened to you in there." Vance leaned against the gate.

"You better check yourself homie." The boy squared his shoulders as he held his cigarette in one hand and his pants with the other.

Vance laughed. "So how you gon' beat me up and you can't even keep your pants up?"

"Don't worry, I won't use my bare hands to handle you." He continued to puff on his cigarette as he pulled up his shirt to show Vance his gun. Vance didn't flinch. He continued leaning against the gate with his arms folded at his chest. "So y'all bold out here like that nowadays? Just ready to shoot up the church, hunh?"

"Naw, I would never disrespect the church like that. That ain't my style, but a fool talking crazy to me, he might get smoked."

Vance pushed himself off the gate with his foot. "I can't tell you got respect for anything or anyone, let alone yourself. You walking around with your pants hanging off of you, smoking a cigarette in front of a church, and carrying a piece. If you weren't so young, I would think you had something to do with my..." Vance let his words trail off hating the fact that day was bringing up so many memories of his past.

The boy had now finished his cigarette. He flicked it off to the side of him into the street.

"Thought I did what?" The boy was curious about what Vance didn't say to him.

"Don't worry about it, so you come every Sunday with your mother?"

The boy's demeanor was now childlike around Vance.

Vance laughed.

"What's so funny dude?" The boy walked closer to Vance.

"I'm confused about why you're here. Why you come every Sunday. I heard what your mother said to you. And I assume you walked out not just because of what she did, but because of what the pastor was saying."

"Yeah, I had to walk out to keep from disrespecting my mother, plus I didn't wanna see her cry again. I get tired of seeing her cry. I knew she knew the pastor was talking about me going down the wrong road. If it ain't her no good boyfriend making her cry then it's me whenever she has to get me out of jail or try to get me back in school."

"So if you don't wanna see her cry, why don't you stop doing whatever it is that keeps getting you into trouble?"

"Man, don't you think I would if I could? I wanna give my momma the world or at least enough to pay the bills and whatnot so she don't have to be with that no good nigga thinking he's the only way she'll survive." The boy turned his back trying to somehow inhale his tears from falling before Vance spotted them.

Vance's heart went out to the boy. "Okay, so you believe the pastor was talking to you? About you?"

The boy laughed and turned back to face Vance confident any trace of him almost crying was gone. "I know he was, must've got all up in yo' business too for you to be out here with me."

"Naw, you can't be affected by what you don't believe in."

The boy's eyebrows furrowed. "Hunh?"

"I don't believe in God. I don't believe in all that crap that guy in there was saying." Vance shoved his hands in his pocket and leaned back against the gate.

The boy distanced himself from Vance. His face contorted as he struggled to find the words to say. "What?" He left his mouth open.

"You heard me."

"Yeah I did. I just don't believe you. So why did you come to church today? It's not like I've seen you here before."

"Well, since my father founded this church, they're honoring his legacy. My mother asked me if I would be here for it today."

"Hunh? Wait." The boy's eyes widened. He held his open hand up waving it at Vance as if requesting time to get his thoughts together. "You're saying you're the late Pastor Sutherland's son?"

"Yup." Vance admired the respect the boy gave his father's legacy.

"Wow. My bad for getting ready to pull my gun out on you earlier." The boy walked over and shook Vance's hand. "Name's Bobby."

"It's cool." Vance smirked sensing the boy wouldn't have used the gun anyway. He picked up on the boy's fake toughness well before the boy shared why he ran the streets.

"Man. I love your mom. She treats me like her grandson or something." Bobby rubbed his face. "Truth be told, she's another reason why I come every Sunday, I feel safe when I'm here." He looked down at the ground.

There was silence between them.

Bobby stared at the way Vance was dressed. He soon turned his back to Vance, pulled his pants up, and adjusted his belt so that it would hold his pants up instead of his hands. He turned back around to face Vance. "Say man, how yo' daddy gon' be who he was, yo' momma who she is, yo' brother who he is, but you be the way you are?" Bobby's eyebrows furrowed.

"What?" Vance laughed.

"I'm saying, from what I hear, your daddy was a powerful man of God. I know your momma hear from God the way she be gettin' on me."

They both laughed.

"And your brother is a cool dude and does a lot around the church all the time, so how come you don't believe in God? That don't make sense to me."

"The same way believing in your God doesn't make sense to me."

"Well, if you did come here to honor your father you better get back in there. I guess I will too."

"You going back in there?" Vance's eyebrows lifted in confusion.

"Yeah, I told you this is the only place I feel safe. I don't know everything there is to know about God, but from the looks of things nowadays, I think it's better to be with Him than without Him."

***

Vance sat at the back of the church again. This time, he hoped it would be for the last time. According to his memory of ceremonies at church, it seemed as if they were finally going to honor his dad. He hoped it would soon be over.

Two hours of God was enough for him and he knew he couldn't bear to sit through the slideshows and whatnot they had prepared to honor his father during the banquet.

He sat baffled that Bobby was sitting next to him again squeezing his mother's hand. He couldn't fathom how Bobby still could believe in God after all he was going through at home and on the streets. He smiled admitting to himself how he could see why Bobby would come to church weekly to see his mother. She had always been a sweet, loving, and caring woman that made anyone she came in contact with feel loved and special.

Pastor Riley interrupted Vance's thoughts. "Ladies and gentlemen, brothers and sisters, it is my honor and privilege to acknowledge the hard work and legacy of the late Pastor Marcus Sutherland Sr."

Everyone stood and clapped.

Vance snarled at the mentioning of his father being deceased. Vance finally stood with the rest of the congregation.

He felt heavy with so much talk of his father going on. He worked hard daily to block out any memories of his father and yet within the almost two hours of being in the church where he grew up in, the part of his heart that he thought he shut down ached.

"I wasn't here when he was and it saddens me that I never had the privilege of meeting the great man you all, this community speaks so highly of...I can only hope I serve this congregation as half as good as he did." Pastor Riley smiled.

"You doing a fine job Pastor Riley. A fine job." A woman shouted out with honey dripping from her voice.

"Well thank you, sister." Pastor Riley avoided making eye contact with the lady. "Not only did this church have the pleasure of Pastor Sutherland founding it and fathering many in it, but even after he has been long gone, the impact of his leadership still lingers heavily around this place."

Vance's jaws clenched. He balled his fists. "If he mentions my daddy being dead one more time, I'mma take him out." Vance didn't care who around him heard.

Fortunately, Bobby was the only one who did.

"Hey man, I heard you. You talked about me needing to change, but it seems like you might need to, too. You can't be up in here threatening Pastor Riley, he's cool. He's one of the ones that cares about us like your father did I guess." Bobby turned his attention back to the pulpit.

Vance was embarrassed. Bobby was right, Pastor Riley seemed to show genuine love to all he came in contact with. Vance reasoned with himself that he couldn't want Bobby to leave the streets alone, but be willing to hurt a guy because of what he was saying.

Vance painfully turned his attention to the pulpit as well.

"....and we thank Mother Sutherland for all she still does day in and day out for this church and this community. She is a wise and elegant woman and we love her."

Everyone stood and cheered.

Vance's mother came and stood at the front of the church where she was ushered to. She was presented with flowers and gift bags.

"And continuing Pastor Sutherland Sr.'s legacy, his son Brother Marcus Jr. has remained faithful serving in the young adult ministry, the men's ministry, and so many other facets of the ministry you all don't know about. From what I hear, he wasn't selfish with his father when he was alive and pastoring in this church and I know personally that he doesn't hold a grudge against me for taking his father's place. So at this time, we want to acknowledge Pastor Sutherland Sr.'s legacy by honoring the imprint his son Marcus Jr. is leaving on this ministry."

Now sitting, the congregation clapped loudly and shouted their 'amens' as Marcus walked up smiling and stood beside his mother. He looked over to his beautiful wife as she sat on the front row to the right of the church, smiling and holding their sleeping infant daughter while their rambunctious two-year son sat near his wife.

"And as many of you all know, this family was a quartet. Pastor Sutherland Sr. and his wife," Pastor Riley smiled at Mother Sutherland, "and his two sons. Like I said, we see Marcus around the church all the time." The congregation laughed. "But today, we have the honor of having the youngest son with us, Brother Vance Sutherland."

The congregation cheered loudly, many of the older congregants whispered to one another. The younger ones never having seen Vance before were surprised to see him. A few single women in the congregation sat upright and lowered the neck of their dresses to reveal more of their cleavage. They each smoothed out their hair and reapplied their lipstick after spying Vance.

Vance was oblivious to the women. He stood and waved his hand hoping that would be enough ceremonious behavior for his appearance, but Pastor Riley signaled for him to come up to the front.

"Brother Vance, come join your family at the front." Pastor Riley smiled.

Vance wanted to curse, but he saw the joy in his mother's eyes as he slowly walked to the front of the church. He dismissed the thought of creating a scene.

A few of the older members that were under Vance's father reached out to shake his hand or give him a kiss on the cheek as he passed them by while some of the others continued to whisper, speculating his whereabouts since his father had died.

Vance shook a few hands and lingered with an elderly woman who he remembered was his favorite church mother. He missed her warm embraces.

"God still has His hand on you baby." Mother Viola's words seemed to somehow unnerve and comfort Vance all at the same time. He knew he had to get out of that place soon. He quickly made it to where his mom and brother were and stood to the right of his mom as the cameras began to flash incessantly.

Pastor Riley continued speaking well of the Sutherland's and all that Pastor Sutherland Sr. had done for the church and the community. "It's obvious how much respect and love you all have for this family from your applause and desire to come up and speak with and hug them, but you can continue that at the banquet immediately following service in the dining hall. Let us all stand and hold hands for the benediction."

The entire congregation stood and held hands with their heads bowed.

"Now may the grace of our Lord rest, rule, reign, and abide in our hearts henceforth and forever more. Let us all say amen."

Many of the members came up to greet the Sutherland's.

Marcus's wife came up and stood by his side as he now held his sleeping baby girl. His wife continued to wrestle with keeping their busy son, Marcus the third under control.

A busty woman approached Vance. "Vance is it?" She didn't even wait for him to respond. "Where have you been? I've only been a member here for two years, but I come every Sunday and I've never seen you." She winked and stood up straighter exposing more of her breasts.

He gave her a half smile not wanting to start a conversation with her. He wanted to kiss his mother and quickly get out of there before Mother Viola or any of the other mothers and deacons spoke to him. "Um, um…" he also wanted to tell her the real reason why she never saw him there, but his mother was too close to him. He hated seeing the pain on her face whenever his lack of belief in her God was brought up. He wished he could make his mother proud in all that he did, but he wouldn't buckle in the area of religion.

Pastor Riley was nearby, knew Vance's story and decided to intervene before any controversy could be birthed from what he might say back to the woman. "Brothers and sisters, remember you'll have a chance to talk with the Sutherland's at the banquet. Now if you'll please make your way downstairs so we can get the banquet started." Pastor Riley nodded to the ushers who in turn started escorting the lines of people away from the Sutherland's.

They all were so eager to share their testimonies of how much Pastor Sutherland had touched their lives.

The women in line waiting to speak with Vance put up a fuss with the ushers before they each surrendered to the ushers directions.

Only Pastor Riley, his wife, the pastor's armor bearer, and Vance and his family were left standing at the altar.

The photographer directed them were to stand and he snapped a few photos of them to commemorate the day.

"Well ma, I'll stop by the house later on this week to see you." Vance reached down and held his mother's shoulders and he kissed her cheek. He loved to be in her presence. She reminded him of better days.

"Vance, please stay." She whispered in her soft voice as a tear rolled down her cheek.

He couldn't see her face, but he heard the angst in her voice.

"Ma, you know why I won't stay." Vance pulled his mother into him. Her face rested on his chest. She was much shorter than him.

Marcus gave his daughter to his wife and then walked over to his mother and rubbed her back.

"Come on, ma. All we can do is continue to pray for him."

Vance laughed. "Pray for me? I'm good. But y'all, y'all need to wake up and see the truth." Vance stepped back and spun around slowly in a circle with his hands outstretched in the air. "Who are you praying to? There is no God. I don't see him. Where is he? He ain't in the pulpit." Vance looked past everyone to the empty chairs on stage. "He ain't in the congregation." He looked behind him at all the empty rows of pews in the church. "He ain't here. He ain't nowhere. He ain't nowhere to be found with all the bad stuff going on in the world. But see, that's the world."

"Vance. Show some respect man." Marcus shouted at his brother.

Vance shook his head at Marcus and continued his rant. "Like I was saying, that's the world, but let me bring it a little closer. Despite what Pastor Riley thinks, He wasn't there when his father killed his momma, his sister, and himself. God's not there for the boy Bobby, who comes here every Sunday but watches his mother get beat by her boyfriend and tricked out to all of the man's friends. And you know what?" Vance screamed admiring his voice echo throughout the massive sanctuary with its tall ceilings and stained glass windows. "He wasn't there when my father," he pointed to himself, " 'our father' " he walked over to Marcus and poked him in the chest and pointed between the two of them, "when 'your husband'," he stopped speaking and caressed his mother's cheek as he held back tears of his own looking at the sadness his rant was evoking in her, but he continued on, " 'the love of your life' was killed. Now an all-knowing, merciful, loving God wouldn't let that happen to His children right? Ain't that what y'all call y'all selves, His children?"

Vance laughed. "Ma, I'm sorry, but you know how I am and that's why I didn't want to be here anyway."

Vance turned to walk away, but his mother began to sing a song his father used to sing before he would preach and it kept him glued to the spot he stood in. "Will your heart and soul say yes?"

His normally soft-spoken mother's voice bellowed throughout the church, inserting guttural groans between lines of the song as she walked towards Vance. "Will your spirit still say yes?"

Although he knew his mother was singing the song, for some odd reason all he could hear was his father's voice singing the words. In the forefront of his mind, he could see his father's eyes, onyx-like, just like his, staring into him while singing the words. Vance shook his head trying to erase the vivid image of his father's piercing voice and eyes staring into him. He tried to will himself to walk, but his mother touched his back and all he could do was fall to his knees.

She pressed against his back still singing the song. She let the Spirit do its work. She sang. "Will your spirit still say yes? There is more that I require of thee, so will your heart and soul say yes?"

Pastor Riley and the others came closer to Vance and his mother and began interceding for Vance.

Vance pounded on the floor under the weight of the Holy Ghost.

"No, I can't trust you." He spoke choking on his tears.

"Now will your heart and soul say yes?" She let each word of the line from the song linger in the air.

The lower Vance neared the floor, the lower Mrs. Sutherland knelt rubbing his back.

"How could you let that happen to my father?"

"There is more that I require of thee…" Mrs. Sutherland continued singing.

The prayers of the others grew louder in the background as they began pacing the floor.

"Why him? He was a good man. I needed him in my life."

The more questions Vance asked, the quieter he got. His body finally relaxed flat on the floor as his mother was now on her knees next to him rubbing his back and head.

The others ended their prayers but quietly began thanking God for what He was doing at that moment.

Silence fell upon the sanctuary.

After time of lying silent on the floor, he slowly rose with his back towards them. He mouthed words. He wiped his face and straightened his suit. He mouthed more words. He turned to face them ready to speak to them, but when he opened his mouth all he could say was 'hallelujah' and 'thank You God'.

He cupped his mouth not believing it came from him, but the words of gratitude continued to flow from his lips until he buckled over with laughter. Tears streamed his face, he stood up straight with his hands lifted high rejoicing in God. He couldn't stop laughing.

Pastor Riley and his wife smiled.

Vance's sister-in-law had to sit to contain her joy. She was so happy knowing how hard and how long Marcus had been praying for this day for Vance.

Marcus ran a few laps around the church expressing his joy to God.

Mrs. Sutherland took her seat on the first row. "He's back, darling." She smiled with her face upright to the ceiling. "He's back home. Thank you God." She wiped her face with her handkerchief.

Every time Vance tried to speak to either of them all he could say was 'thank You God'. He took a seat at the end of a pew nearby and lowered his head in his hands trying to compose himself. He sat there for quite some time smiling with his head low and mumbling.

He finally stood up, straightened out his suit, smoothed down his hair, and walked over to his beaming brother. They stared at each other silently for a moment before smiles covered their faces. They gave each other a fist bump before Marcus pulled Vance into him and gave him a bear hug. "Thanks man for not giving up on me." Vance said to his brother.

"I never could and I never will. We're Sutherland men, and as dad used to say, 'we're built Ford tough.' "

Vance playfully pushed Marcus away from him and turned to Pastor Riley. He stepped up to him and shook his hand. "I'm sorry Pastor Riley for my display a minute ago." Vance held Pastor Riley's hand firmly.

"No need to apologize. I'm happy for what came after it." Pastor Riley smiled and while still holding Vance's right hand pulled him into a manly embrace.

Vance pulled back from Pastor Riley but still firmly gripped his hand. "I know this is my first time meeting you, being here in a loooong time, but from what I've seen today, you're doing a fine job here. Good preaching too." Vance laughed.

"I would love to have you here working in whatever capacity you would like to." Pastor Riley smiled.

Vance smirked. "Let me think about that." Vance turned and walked towards his mother. He paused to embrace his sister-in-law and then kissed his niece and nephew before he took a seat next to his mother.

Then others stood in a huddle talking.

"Momma," he wrapped his arm around her as she sat there smiling and basking in the ray of sunlight that now beamed on both of them.

She looked at him. "I'm so proud of you."

The warmth in her voice let Vance know it was his cue to leave. He thought he had done enough crying for the day, but his mother's joy was stirring more tears in him.

She continued to speak, "God never left you."

Vance nodded. "I know momma." A lump formed in his throat.

"You know your father is rejoicing in heaven right now."

Tears flowed from his eyes. For the first time in a long time, the mention of his father brought joy to his heart. The flood of memories racing through his head of his father made him smile. He squeezed his mother tighter. "I know momma."

"Good, well then, let's go eat," she spoke as she stood to her feet along with Vance's help. Her grandson rushed to her side. "I'm hungry too, nana." They all laughed as Marcus the third stood by her side. Everyone walked towards the exit headed to the dining hall except for Vance.

"Bruh, I know it's been a long time since you've been here, but we gotta go this way to get to the food," Marcus said.

"I know." Vance looked back smiling at Marcus.

"Well then come on."

"Naw, I can't go to the banquet."

They all looked worried as if he had somehow lost his way with God again so soon.

Marcus, with a pensive look on his face, walked slowly towards Vance. "Why not?"

"Because if those women who were waiting in line for me earlier are down there, then I don't need to be."

Marcus's eyebrows furrowed. "What? Why not?"

"Because I'm not trying to be what they eat. They looked like they wanted to devour me." Vance laughed and everyone joined in laughing with him.

"Well Bro. Vance, I can't argue with you on that one." Pastor Riley shook his head. "Will I see you again?"

"Yes sir, you will." Vance responded to Pastor Riley. "Marcus, just make me a plate. I'll pick it up from your house later."

"Whatever." Marcus responded laughing as he picked his son up and headed to the exit with the others.

Vance made it to the entrance of the church. He opened the doors and the sun was still shining. It felt like God was still talking to him. He stood still and silent taking in what had happened to him over the last hour. He was grateful to be back on track with God, but as he walked to his car, he couldn't help but remember the worry in his heart about where he stood with Pam.

22

Pam walked in her front door and closed it after herself. She let out a deep breath as she fell back against the door. "Lord, give me the strength to make it to my bed." She laughed at herself and then used her foot to kick herself off the door and make her way into her bedroom.

She dropped her bags on the floor of her bedroom and dived into her soft bed she remembered Kim said she wanted to steal from her.

She missed her friends dearly, but she surmised she would have to see them another day because the only thing that was on her agenda at that moment was to sleep until she had no choice but to get up and get ready for her return to work the next day.

Within minutes, her room was filled with her snoring. She slept for all of five minutes before her phone and doorbell rang at the same time. She rolled over on her bed hoping to shake her head of the dream where everything was ringing but when knocks hit her door, she knew she was no longer dreaming.

Groggy, she slowly got up out of her bed and headed to her front door. She was too tired to get on her tip toes to look out the peep hole, so she let her forehead drop on the door with her arms dangling at her sides. "Who is it?" She tried to speak loudly, but exhaustion had a strong grip on her vocal chords.

"Who do you think it is? Open up this door."

"Kim, go away. I just need to sleep. I'll see you at work in the morning." Pam willed herself off of the door and drug her feet back towards her room.

There was more banging at the door.

"Pam, Kim isn't the only one here, it's all of us." Monica said.

"Ugh." Pam turned around and unlocked her door and then headed back to her bedroom. She knew the ladies wouldn't leave until they saw her face to face. This time when she made it to her room, she mustered up enough strength to get under her covers.

"You better had let us in." Kim laughed as she entered. She went straight to the kitchen to raid the refrigerator while Monica and Renee made their way into Pam's room.

Renee and Monica found comfy spots on the floor and in the oversized chair in the room.

Pam snored.

Kim entered the room smacking on chips. "You never have any good stuff."

"And you never ask before you raid someone's kitchen." Renee noted.

"I never will. Real friend code." Kim snapped back.

They all laughed except for Pam, who was asleep.

"Pam. Pam. Get up." Kim stood over Pam.

"You see she's asleep. We should have checked with her before we just showed up anyway." Monica chimed in.

"Uh, no. Her track record with getting back to us this past year has been horrible. I didn't want to take that chance." Kim plopped down on the bed hoping it would wake Pam.

Pam didn't budge.

"We just left the hospital. Her dad did say that she's been tending to her mother day in and day out. This is her first day back home. She needs this rest. Let's go." Renee said.

Kim cocked her head in Monica and Renee's direction. "I swear, sometimes y'all act like y'all never met me. Now y'all know I'm not leaving from here until I tell her what I need to tell her and make sure she's alright." Kim bucked her eyes especially at Renee and then turned her attention back to Pam. She shook Pam awake. "Get up girl. Get up girl. I know you're tired, so the sooner you get up and talk to us, the sooner you can get back to sleep." Kim laughed as she leaned down to kiss Pam's cheek. "I've missed you, my friend." Crumbs from Kim's mouth dropped on Pam's face.

"Eww." Pam sat up pushing Kim off of her. "You messed up a mushy moment with your greedy self."

They all laughed.

"I don't know where all that junk that you eat goes with as svelte as you are."

"Well thank you, my dear." Kim stood up and spun in a circle showcasing her toned body.

Her physique matched her energetic and outgoing spirit. Her height peaked at five feet and three inches and she weighed about a hundred and thirty-five pounds. She had caramel coated skin with dimpled chubby cheeks and round doe eyes. Kim was very fashionable and always kept up with the latest trends.

"Sit down somewhere." Renee said shaking her head.

"You're just jealous that you don't look like me." Kim stuck her tongue out at Renee.

"Kim, actually she does, remember, she is your triplet." Pam said and they all laughed except for Kim.

"Oh shut up." Kim flopped down on the bed again. "She may favor me, but she doesn't look exactly like me, and she definitely doesn't flaunt it like me."

"You're right, I don't look like you and I don't want to." Renee scrunched up her face.

"Alright now you too. Don't start. My toddler twins are better behaved than you two." Monica said.

"Not when I get done with them." Kim laughed. "Anywho, Pam," she turned her attention to Pam, "how have you really been doing?"

Pam sat up against her tufted headboard. "I'm good."

"Your mom looked good for recently having had two seizures and brain surgery within the last two weeks." Monica came and got in the bed next to Pam.

Pam pointed her finger to the ceiling. "But God."

"Yes, God." Renee came over to sit at the edge of the bed.

"Yes, I can agree that it was no one but God that brought your mother through this." Kim said.

Everyone looked at her in amazement.

"What? Y'all gon' stop acting like I'm a heathen. I believe in God like y'all do. And guess who else does too now?" Kim winked at Pam and bounced on the bed.

Pam sat upright. "What? Who?" Kim had Pam's mind racing.

"You can tell her about that later. Let's first make sure she's okay with her mother." Monica reminded Kim.

"Alright, alright." Kim frowned.

"No, tell me who now." Pam pouted.

"Monica's right, I'll save that for last. When we last talked to you, you told us that your mother had another seizure at the hospital while you all were having an argument." Kim said.

Monica noted Pam's sadness and rubbed her hand for comfort.

Renee scooted up to rub Pam's feet through the cover.

Kim continued to eat chips waiting for Pam to speak.

"Yeah, I know I haven't been able to talk to you all since that day. I've been making up for lost time with my mom."

"Do tell." Kim said.

"Well, as I told you all, she had a seizure again because her blood pressure rose too high during our convo."

"What exactly were you talking about that got her so heated?"

"Dang Kim, would you quit smacking on those chips and let Pam finish. You know she'll tell us if you just shut up."

Kim looked back at Renee and rolled her eyes but then laughed.

"Y'all are a mess." Pam laughed but continued talking. "Well, you all know my relationship with my mother has always been strained. I never felt that closeness with her that you and Renee have with your mom." She looked at Kim. "I even felt closer to your mom than my own for the longest. Oddly, my mom knew about my affair with Steve before you all did." Pam hung her head.

"What?" Monica scooted closer to Pam.

"Yeah, when I was staying with my parents, I needed to talk to someone about it and I guess I let it slip out with her, but I regretted it immediately the minute she started in on me. Well, the day she was in the hospital recovering after her surgery, we were talking and she told me she didn't think I would be by her side through it all because she thought I didn't like her. I decided to be honest with her about how I felt when she shared her feelings with me. As I was letting her know exactly how I felt, she started seizing. It scared the crap out of me knowing how fragile she still was at that time and then to have it happen again, I knew it was my fault that time. Well the doctors handled the seizure and no damage was done to her neurologically. After her seizure in the hospital, my father suggested that I not bring any of the convo up we were having that day, but when she felt up to talk, she insisted that we continue the convo."

They all looked to Kim waiting for her to ask a question.

"What? I said I would listen this time." She laughed and continued chewing on the chips. "Although I am thirsty now, can you hold your next thought?"

They laughed as Kim rushed from the room to get a cup of juice and ran back into the room.

"Okay, you may continue."

They all stared at her.

"What?" Kim asked looking at each of them.

"You didn't even ask if we wanted something to drink." Monica said.

"Because you all know where the kitchen is and how to get it yourself, especially you," she looked at Pam. "You live here. Duh." Kim laughed as the others shook their heads at her.

"As I was saying," Pam paused looking at Kim chomp on the last of the chips in the bag, "she basically told me that she really does love me. She said she's always wanted to be closer to me than we've been but because of the choices I've made in life, she didn't always agree with them. She said she guess she let her feelings about my decisions for my life dictate how she interacted with me."

Renee smiled. "I bet you were happy about that weren't you?"

"Yes." Pam's smile grew. "It was like gaining a new friend. I know she's my mom and I won't share everything with her, but it feels good to know that I can go to her about stuff and she promised not to judge and condemn me but be a listening ear and talk me through things if need be. I was enjoying her company so much that I didn't want to leave."

"I bet your dad was happy about your new relationship with your mom too wasn't he?" Monica asked.

"Yup. He and I have always been close, and of course, he wanted that for me and her. He's always told me that my mom loves me and wanted the best for me, she just showed it in a different way. I finally see that now." Pam sat back against her headboard squeezing a pillow near her chest and smiled.

"Awww Pam, you're melting my heart." Kim laughed reaching out to cup Pam's face.

Pam laughed as she ducked Kim's hand and hit Kim with a pillow.

"Now you know you don't want to start a fight with the pillow fight queen." A look of determination beamed in Kim's eyes.

Renee held her hands up in the air in protest. "No, we don't want your overly competitive tail to do anything but stay calmly seated." Renee and Monica laughed.

"That's because y'all know I'll beat y'all." Kim laughed.

"Whatever Kim." Monica looked to Pam, "so your mom is okay now or at least on the road to a smooth recovery, right?"

"Yes, we have to keep her from being the busy body that she loves to be until the doctor fully clears her." Pam smiled. "I'm totally happy with where she and I stand now. I didn't want to leave her, so I slept at the hospital with her every night, but my dad reminded me that she's his wife. He said he'd been married to her long enough to know how to take care of her, she would be in perfectly good hands with him, and that I needed to get back home, back to my life, my students. I agreed and he sent me on my way. So I'm home now trying to sleep before I have to get ready for my first day back at work tomorrow, but y'all won't let me." Pam laughed.

"Nope, not until we made sure that everything is okay with your mom and you."

"Well, it is, so good night." Pam scooted down in her bed and pulled the covers over her head.

"Um, we're not done with you yet." Kim pulled the covers back from over Pam.

"You are such a pest." Pam snarled at Kim.

"But you still love me anyway, so that's all that matters." Kim retorted.

They all laughed.

"So, while you were busy rebuilding your relationship with your mom, guess who was busy rebuilding their relationship with God?"

Pam perked up. "Who? Stop stalling. Tell me already. The who and what you're hinting at has been playing in my head since you first brought up the 'news' you have to tell me." Pam now sat Indian style staring at Kim.

Kim stood up. "Well, it's a he. He's tall, chocolate covered skin, dark eyes, big bright smile, very articulate, muscular." Kim accentuated each word she said with her hands.

Renee and Monica sat laughing at Kim's gestures and the look of cluelessness on Pam's face.

Kim looked at Pam still not knowing who she was talking about. She wanted to give clues for Pam to say his name before she flat out told her who it was. "Let's see, he drives a Ford Mustang, he's definitely educated, has a job, a good paying reputable job."

Renee and Monica laughed loudly at Kim and Pam's exchange of looks at one another.

Pam jumped out of her bed and pounced onto Kim. She gripped Kim's shoulders and staring into Kim's eyes she spoke. "Would you stop with the charades and tell me already."

Kim buckled over in laughter and Pam laughed as she returned to her bed.

"Oh, you've always sucked at the guessing game. I'm talking about our boss, Mr. Sutherland, Vance." Kim sat back down on the bed waiting to see how her revelation would hit Pam.

Pam leaned back against the headboard again. "Vance? Rebuilt his relationship with God? Our boss? The one who I told you is an atheist? That Vance?" Pam's eyebrows wrinkled.

"Yes, that Vance you just described." Kim nodded her head.

Pam looked to Monica and Renee for clarity. They both nodded their heads in agreement.

Renee spoke up. "That's what she told us as soon as she found out."

"They weren't there, I was." Kim said.

"And how did you find this out? He told you himself?" Pam asked.

"Not quite." Kim said.

"So you don't know for sure then?"

"I believe I do." Kim said.

"How so?" Pam said.

"Well see, apparently he rededicated his life back to God the Sunday your mom had her second seizure. From what Shelly shared with me one day I was in the office inquiring about the new pep in his step, she told me everything. That Sunday, his dad's church was honoring his father as the founder and spiritual leader of the church and neighborhood."

Pam sat still clinging to every word Kim said.

"As told to Shelly by Vance himself, he didn't want to be there because of his non-beliefs at the time because how he felt God forsook his father by letting him get killed."

Pam's eyes widened. Her mouth gaped open.

"Clearly you didn't know that, but anywho, because he promised his mom he would, he was there. Well after a few encounters with people that day, especially the Holy Spirit, his words to Shelly, not mine, he accepted Christ as his Lord and Savior again."

"Wow. I didn't know that was his reason for his not believing in God, but I'm glad he surrendered himself to God again." Pam leaned back against her headboard smiling in shock.

"I know right. So now this means that you too can finally get together." Renee perked up.

Monica propped pillows behind her back to get more comfortable.

Pam frowned as she pulled a pillow closer to her and squeezed it tightly. "I doubt that."

"Why?" Renee asked.

"Well, I'm glad, I'm really excited that he rededicated his life to God, but I think with how many times and the ways I've treated him awfully, I doubt if he'll ever find me attractive again."

"I highly doubt that." Kim lifted her chin in the air. I'm convinced that any man that gets even a whiff of the four of us can't leave us alone." Kim laughed.

The others shook their heads.

"I mean really, Keith loved Monica from the day he met her back in middle school."

Monica smiled. "Yeah, my honey did."

"And you know the guys I deal with can't get enough of me."

"You're so full of yourself." Renee said to Kim.

Pam and Monica shook their heads laughing.

"And you, if you weren't so gangly, I think a man would even find you admirable." Kim looked over her shoulder at Renee.

Renee's face winced. "I happen to like my look, thank you very much. And besides, I've never had a problem getting a guy to like me, that's just not my focus now."

"Yeah, that's what you say." Kim laughed.

Renee hit Kim with a pillow.

"Alright now, don't start with me, remember I am the queen of pillow wars." Kim pointed her finger at Renee.

Pam and Monica shook their heads laughing at the sisters.

"Seriously Pam, the way he seemed to be feeling you, I doubt there is anything you could do to make him not like you anymore." Kim spoke.

"I don't know guys, seems like every time I see him I say and do more that would seem to push him away. Looking back, although I wasn't myself that day, I'm embarrassed to admit how I talked to him the day he took me to the hospital when my mom fell. That was the last time we talked."

The others sat quietly noting how somber Pam was.

"Well, you go back to work tomorrow so we shall see. And on that note and since everything has been discussed that needed to be discussed, I think we can officially leave now." Kim said.

Pam frowned. "Really. I was getting comfortable with you all being here now. I've missed you all."

Monica stood up from the bed and stretched. "We've missed you too, but Kim's right for a change, it's time to go."

Kim rolled her eyes at Monica and then laughed.

"I need to get home to all of my babies, especially my husband." Monica winked.

"Ugh!" Kim and Renee said in unison.

"Would you stop talking about our brother like that around us." Kim pretended to gag.

"Nope." Monica laughed.

Pam got out of her bed to walk her friends to the door.

They all hugged before Kim, Renee, and Monica stepped into the hallway.

"Thank you guys for being such great friends, sisters, and checking up on me."

"We wouldn't have it any other way." Renee smiled.

"Bye." They walked towards the stairs.

"Wait, before you all go."

They turned to look back at Pam.

"How in the heck do you all keep getting in my building without me buzzing you all in?"

Kim spoke up. "Again, don't act like you don't know me, I have my ways." Kim winked. "And oh sweetie, if you really do wanna make a good impression on the boss tomorrow upon returning, make sure you spruce yourself up. I know you've been busy tending to your mom and all, but take a look in the mirror and figure out what you need to do before you show up at work in the a.m." Kim gave Pam a half smile.

"Kim, you are so rude." Renee hit Kim on her arm.

"Nah, just keeping it real with my girl. I love her like that."

"You are something else." Pam laughed as she closed her door.

She went to the bathroom and looked at herself in the mirror. Kim was right, she needed to do some fine tuning to herself in preparation for her return to work the next day.

She knew it wouldn't take much elbow grease to look her best; she simply wasn't sure what she would say to Vance the next day, better yet, what to do with her feelings for him.

23

Pam returned to work that Monday morning. She stood in the hallway with the other teachers on the floor ready to greet the students as the students walked the halls headed to their classrooms.

"Ms. Robinson, you're back." Sharday ran up to her and hugged her.

She squeezed Sharday as hard as Sharday squeezed her. She missed her kids, especially the one hugging her.

"I'm glad to be back. Look at you. Smiling all hard and all. Is everything okay?"

"Yes it is. Asia really is my friend now."

"Good. Glad to hear that. Okay, now go to your seat and get ready for the day."

Sharday walked into the classroom as Pam greeted the rest of her class.

After seeing that all of her students were in the classroom, Pam walked in and closed the door behind her.

Michael stood up. "Ms. Robinson?"

"Yes, Michael?" She smiled at him and leaned back against her desk. She took note of the silence in the classroom.

"Well, after two weeks of you being gone, we made Mr. Sutherland tell us why you hadn't been here. And when he told us, we decided to make some 'get well' cards for your mom. We even made a few 'I'm sorry' cards for you too."

The kids began to bring up the cards they made for her and hugged her. Her eyes misted more and more seeing the beautiful and thoughtful handmade cards the kids had made for her.

After the last student returned to his seat, Pam spoke as she wiped her eyes. "Thank each and every one of you all for these beautiful cards." She folded her arms at her chest holding the cards close to the center of her chest.

She walked behind her desk to get to her computer to take attendance.

Michael spoke up again. "Ms. Robinson?"

"Yes, Michael?" she looked up to him.

"How's your mom?"

"Michael, we're not supposed to ask her," Asia said.

Pam laughed. "No, it's okay Asia. I imagined you all would want to know how she's doing anyway. Let me finish taking attendance and doing the lunch count then I'll update you all." Pam laughed inwardly noting that Asia could still be sassy when she needed to be.

They all sat quietly eager to hear about Pam's mother.

She pressed submit on the screen and then scooted closer under her desk to talk to the kids. She scanned the room looking at each of them before she spoke. She was hoping the looks of innocence on their faces would ground her and keep her from getting emotional as she retold what happened. She didn't plan to share all, just enough to hopefully satisfy their curiosity. "Well, my mother fell and had a seizure which required her to have emergency brain surgery..."

Vance stood out of view in the hallway not wanting to interrupt her summation to her students, but he could still hear her voice through the door loud and clear. He hated to eavesdrop on his teachers, but to hear her voice at that moment comforted the longing he had in his heart for her.

"She was on the road to recovery, but she had another seizure." Pam continued.

The kids gasped.

"It's okay. The second one wasn't as bad as the first one. If she continues to progress the way she is, she'll be getting released soon. Luckily she won't need any speech therapy or anything like that. Thank you all so much for being so concerned about my mom and me, but now it's time for you all to line up for music."

"Well, we're glad she's okay and you're back." Michael said.

"Thank you. I'm glad to be back."

"Good because we only have like a week of school left and we want to spend it with you, our favorite teacher." Sharday said.

"Aw, that's so sweet. Okay, girls line up. Boys line up."

"Yeah, Ms. Davis, the substitute was cool after she stopped being so mean." Michael laughed and all the kids joined in with him.

Pam walked into the hallway with her students and noticed that Vance was standing at the other door to her classroom.

He gave her a half smile.

The kids waved at him as they walked past him.

Pam stopped to speak to him. "Did you need something from me?" She searched his eyes for a clue of how he felt for her. She hated the emotions that were running through her heart and mind about him. She always found him attractive but thought nothing could ever become of them because she knew they weren't equally yoked. However, now that she knew he was of the same faith as her and they could actually get together, the thought of him possibly not wanting her anymore annoyed her.

"Uh, yeah," he didn't stare into her eyes as he normally did. "I see you're taking the kids to music now, so stop by my office when you can. Welcome back." He walked away.

With a newly saddened attitude, Pam directed her class to music.

***

Pam walked into the main office. "Is he in his office?" She pointed to Vance's office door but spoke to Shelly.

"Yeah, he's in there. Let me see if he's available." Shelly smiled and dialed Vance's phone. "He's on the phone, but he said you can come in."

Pam stepped into Vance's office.

He signaled her to close the door behind her.

When she did so, he stood while still on the phone and mouthed to her to have a seat.

He sat down after she did so.

"Okay. Thank you, sir. I'll get back to you by the end of the day...Okay, you too. Have a great day." Vance hung up the phone and looked at Pam. "Sorry, I had to take that call."

"It's okay. You're a busy man running this school and all." Pam smiled as she made sure her skirt was past her knees. She crossed her legs at her ankles and then tucked them under the seat. "You said you needed to see me." Pam's eyebrows raised as she looked at nothing particular in the office.

"Yes." He leaned forward on the desk clasping his hands together. "First, I want to ask, how is your mom?"

"She's doing fine. It'll be a while before she's fully back to herself, but we all expect her to have a full recovery."

"Thank God." Vance said.

Despite what Kim had already told her, Pam was still shocked when Vance acknowledged God. She cleared her throat and shifted in her seat before she spoke again "Yes, nobody but God did it for her."

Vance gave her a sincere smile.

"The other thing I wanted to do is to apologize for my behavior or anything that I may have said over the past months that may have rubbed you the wrong way."

"No need for you to apologize, in fact, I need to apologize to you for my behavior-"

"I'm sorry to cut you off, and I apologize for bringing this up here and now, it's just that the last time we spoke, we saw each other, it ended not so well, and I want to make sure that our professional relationship is still in tact."

Pam swallowed his last words hard.

"I see how I overstepped my boundaries with you trying to see if there was more to us than just co-workers and friends, but time and time again you told me it wouldn't work out. I respect your decision. Again, I apologize, I'm sorry, it won't happen again." Vance stood up hoping his heart would catch up with what he said to Pam.

Taking the cue from Vance, Pam stood as well. "Vance," she looked at the stoic look on face, "Mr. Sutherland, I...I...I" She didn't even know what to say at that moment. His demeanor was so standoffish to her and he refused to look her in her eyes. She couldn't tell if his eyes said otherwise than what his mouth spoke.

She turned and walked towards the door.

He followed behind her. He grabbed the doorknob to open it.

Pam turned around to face him. She looked up into his eyes.

He finally looked into her eyes. He hated the sadness he saw in them because of what he said to her, but he knew it was only so much rejection and back and forth he could take from her. He mainly wanted to focus on rebuilding his relationship with God. He had no choice but to believe that love would come to him when the time was right and the right woman came along for him.

Pam's eyes misted. Her mouth was dry. Still staring into his eyes, smelling the inebriating scent of his cologne, and feeling the closeness of his body to hers, she parted her lips to speak but nothing came out. She pursed her lips tight and faced the door again waiting for him to open it for her.

He leaned forward, twisted the knob, and held the door open as she walked past him.

Pam rushed to her classroom to be alone. She felt such a finality with Vance in his office moments ago that she cursed ever coming to the school, ever looking into his eyes only to see how much she cared for him.

She couldn't wait for the school year to be over. "I might transfer to another school." She sat at her desktop and opened up the site showing her teacher openings at other schools in the district.

***

Pam left the building late that day grading papers and trying to catch up on lesson plans.

She was thankful that when she clocked out Vance wasn't in the office. She wouldn't mind not seeing him for a while. Maybe not doing so would heal her heart a lot quicker.

She admitted to herself how fond she was of him with so many spoken and unspoken powerful and magnetic moments between them that she had come to treasure. Pam looked back thinking that if there was ever such a thing as a soul mate, Vance may be hers.

I thought I loved Steve, but clearly that wasn't love. The way I feel about Vance now makes me wonder is this how love should feel? My feelings for him are stronger than like, because the bummed out way I feel at that moment is so much worse than my heartbreak over Steve. Looking back now, I see I lusted after Steve, but my feelings for Vance are sincere. Steve? Why did Steve pop up in mind? But thank God he's out of my life now. Pam smiled at that thought.

She opened the back door of the school. She walked towards her car, but with the sun beaming on her car, all she could see was the silhouette of a man leaning on her car. She walked towards her car cautiously looking around her to see if anyone else was in the parking lot and would be able to aid her if she needed help. Pam reached for her purse to grab her mace but realized she never switched it over from the purse she carried while staying in the hospital with her mother.

She was tired and wanted to get home and the only way she could do that was to get the strange man away from her car and she speed off in it. She threw caution to the wind and kept walking to her car. About an arm's length from her car the sun seemed to settle away from her car and she was able to see the face of the man leaning against her car.

It was Steve.

She snarled. "What are you doing here? Please step away from my car." She pushed him aside as she pressed the unlock button on her key.

"Here let me help you with that?" Steve reached out to take some of her bags from her.

She nearly toppled over flailing her arms trying to keep him from touching her. She lost her balance and landed butt first on the ground.

He tried not to laugh at her, but she was so cute to him flustered and all. "I tried to help you but you wouldn't let me." He reached out his hand to help her up.

She refused it. She released all of the bags still in her hand and managed to stand up. She dusted her clothes and hands off. "Get away."

"No. I had to come check up on you. Asia told me that you hadn't been to work in two weeks. I got worried. I had no number to reach you at. You blocked me from all of your social media accounts and I don't have your new address. I talked to her after school and she told me you were back and that your mom was okay. I had to come see you for myself. Sorry, but this is the only place I knew I could reach you at. Don't you see that it's fate that brought us back together? I mean, who would've thought that you would end up being my daughter's teacher and that I could be in contact with you on the regular if you'll let me."

"The devil himself." Pam said as she put all of her bags in the trunk of her car. She closed it and walked back to her driver's side door, but he blocked it.

He laughed. "No, it's fate sweetheart."

"Steve, move out of my way." She stood flat footed in front of him, nostrils flaring and her hands on her hips."

He laughed. "You know your pouting is only making me want you more, right? You used to pout all the time when you didn't want me to leave you at night, it worked then and it's working now. Let's say we go somewhere else and talk. Maybe back to your place?" Steve smirked and winked at Pam.

She stepped closer to him. "You are a bigger fool than I thought you were if you think that I want any more to do with you."

Steve stood unfazed by her words.

Vance had stepped outside of the building and was headed to his car. He could see Pam talking to a man at her car, but he knew they couldn't see him from the shadow he stood in.

"Steve move out of my way now."

"Look Pammie-"

"Don't call me that." Pam shot daggers with her eyes at Steve.

"But you used to love when I called you that when we made love." He reached both of his hands out to grab her waist trying to pull her closer to him, but she slapped both of them away from him.

Vance dropped his briefcase but stood in place. He needed his hands-free in case he had to run over to help Pam again.

Pam stepped back and away from Steve.

"Steve, I don't want anything to do with you anymore, so please leave me alone. Asia is doing fine in class. If I ever need to talk to one of her parents again, I'll contact your wife-"

"Ex-wife." Steve corrected her.

Pam stood with her arms crossed at her chest with her fists balled. She had one foot distanced in front of the other. She was in fight stance and ready to defend herself if need be.

"Calm down, Pam. You're grinding your teeth so hard they may crumble." Steve laughed. "I swear, I promise," he raised his right hand in the air, "I am not here to make you feel uncomfortable or anything like that. I really miss you. I would've never stopped pursuing you, but I figured after the last time we saw each other, you needed some time to calm down, remember what we had. I do and I want it back. Matter of fact I want it better than before." Steve relaxed his body against her car, crossed his ankles, and folded his arms at his chest. His stare at her intensified with admiration.

Pam raised her finger to speak, but he silenced her.

"And before you say anything else, here." He reached into his back pocket and handed Pam some folded papers.

She furrowed her eyebrows looking at his hand holding the papers.

He laughed. "I want you to take a look at them." He placed them in her hand.

"I don't care what's on those papers, I want you to get out of my way so I can go."

"Would you please look at them?" Steve smiled.

Hoping it would hurry him away from her, Pam snatched the papers from him and opened them. At the top it read 'Stephen Brown is hereby granted a divorce to Angel Brown on this day April 13, 2015.'

He smiled as she recognized what the papers were. "You see. I'm a free man. So you and I can start over. Start our lives together." Steve was hopeful.

"Haaa! You are a nut if you think that I want to start anything with you." Pam took a deep breath. She realized that in that moment she had no desire to ever be with him again. There was no need for her to feel so tense around him. Her shoulders relaxed and she smiled. She reached out and grabbed his hand and nicely placed the divorce papers back into his. Her smile grew wider thinking about how free her heart was of him.

Vance took note of how relaxed Pam seemed with the man now and that she was smiling with him. He recognized him as the parent who had Pam in a frenzy weeks ago, but now she was so calm around him. Vance didn't know what they were saying, but whatever it was it now seemed like Pam was entertained by the guy. He didn't want to interfere with Pam's life anymore. *She's a grown woman. She doesn't look like she's in danger now.*

She was taking care of herself before I met her...I guess she'll be fine without me. He reached down and picked up his briefcase and started the walk to his car.

Pam looked Steve straight in his eyes as she smiled. "Stephen Brown, please know that there isn't a nerve ending in my body that tingles at the mere thought of you. I don't hate you, but I definitely don't love you anymore and there will never be an *us* again. I'm glad that you're divorce is final and I hope that you treat the next woman right. Despite how you deceived me and your wife, I pray that no one ever hurts you and treats you the way you did myself and your wife. I pray that you find the peace of God to move on in life." Pam smiled.

Vance looked over again to see how serene Pam's face was talking to the guy. *Maybe he's the reason why she didn't want me. Maybe she only acted that way with him in front of me and this is how she is with him, all happy and all. I guess it's best that I really do move on.* Vance looked up for a second and locked eyes with Pam. The look in his eyes was as far away from her as the physical distance between them. Pam felt a sting in her heart.

She wished she could run over to talk to him but she needed to finish what was in front of her.

Vance put his briefcase in his backseat. He quickly got into his driver's seat, started his car and sped off not wanting to see Pam possibly kiss the guy.

Pam allowed her eyes to follow Vance's car until it was no longer in sight. She shook her head before returning her attention to Steve. "And *you* must move now. You're blocking my way."

Steve had never heard Pam speak to him with such calm authority. The tranquil look in her eyes let him know that what they had was definitely over. He stood to his feet and off of her car as he threw his hands in the air as if in defeat. "Okay Pam. Seems like you've made up your mind. I guess I have no choice but to respect that. Here's my new number and address in case you decide to change your mind." Steve tried handing Pam a note he had pre-written his info on.

She looked down at it. "No thanks, I won't be needing it."

Steve backed up and allowed Pam to get in her car.

She drove out of the parking lot leaving Steve standing there.

She worked hard to concentrate driving home thinking about the last look she saw in Vance's eyes, it was one of defeat and goodbye.

24

Despite everything that happened during the course of the year, Pam had honestly enjoyed her school year and hated that it had come to an end in what seemed such a short time. She liked her class that year and was sad that she would no longer interact with them the next school year, but she was sure that she would gel well with the next group of students placed in her class. She would make it her duty.

As tradition, Vance hosted an end of the year cookout to show his appreciation for the faculty and staff's hard work throughout the school year.

It was a beautiful day outside. The sun was shining brightly. The birds were chirping and the flowers in the school's garden provided a beautiful array of colors as a backdrop for where the cookout was stationed in the parking lot.

Luckily for the staff, Vance's committee had put most of the tables underneath trees to shade them from the blazing sun.

Pam was allowing her hair to grow back and since it was now hot daily and she didn't want to have to deal with styling her own hair every day, she decided to get micro braids as a protective style for her hair for the summer.

She sat at a table in the shade wearing a deep purple sleeveless sundress with gold and silver sandals adorning her feet. She wore silver accessories that complemented her chocolate skin well. She was lost in her thoughts recounting how close her and her mother continued to grow daily since the seizures and the brain surgery. She thanked God daily that He allowed her mother to come through it and mended their relationship to be what it was. She couldn't wait to stop by and see her mom later on that evening. She enjoyed the quality time she was spending with her mom and dad. She especially loved when her brothers came over with their wives and kids. She could only pray to be patient enough until the time came when she would be there with her husband and children with the rest of her family.

She sat there quietly thinking about Vance when Kim interrupted her thoughts as she walked over to her table.

"Pam, hey girl. It took me a minute to find you, but I did." Kim took her seat with a plate full of food. She looked Pam up and down before she spoke again. "Mmm hmm, who are you trying to impress looking as pretty as you do?"

Pam laughed and shook her head. "Myself, girl."

"If that's what you want to say out loud, but I know the truth." Kim replied blissfully knowing it would spark up the "Vance" conversation.

"And what 'truth' do you think you know?" Pam asked already anticipating Kim's response.

"Lean in closer so that you can hear me real good." Kim stopped chewing to make sure Pam understood every word she said. "You still want Mr. Sutherland and I know he wants you." Kim stuck her fork into the spaghetti on her plate. She wound it around the fork before putting it up to her mouth. She eyed Pam speechless before she slurped what was on her fork. She laughed

"Girl, whatever. That is so over." Pam spoke looking across the lot at Vance sitting and talking with a group of his friends.

"I don't know who you think you're talking to. You know good and well I know you and that you are lying. A blind dog could see that you all still like each other."

"A blind dog. Really?" Pam laughed.

"Yes, a blind dog. I swear, if the rest of the staff paid more attention to how awkward you all are around each other, they would agree with me. Y'all try to be professional with one another, but it comes across like two band geeks dating for the first time ever. Neither one knows what to do when they are around the other." Kim bit into a chicken wing. Juice from it dripped from her mouth. She rushed to grab a napkin to clean up the potential mess. "I tell you what, I wish y'all would get together, he can really cook. I would stay at y'all house eating."

Pam shook her head as Kim scooped up baked beans and shoved them in her mouth.

"What, I shut you up with the truth?" Kim laughed and finally pushed her plate away.

"No, however, I know you well enough to know you won't stop talking about something until you're good and ready."

"You're right about that, and this conversation my friend, won't end until I give the toast at you all's wedding reception."

"Haaa." Pam laughed hard as she sat with her face in her hands. She worked hard to avoid looking in Vance's direction. The sun kissing his chocolate skin ignited her fantasies of them being together.

"Knock it off with this woe is me vibe you have going on right now. He's saved now, so there's a very strong chance that you two could end up together."

Pam sighed. She angled her head to look at Kim. "Just because we're 'equally yoked' now doesn't mean that we'll automatically be together. He has to want to be with me for that to happen." Pam felt her stomach growling with hunger.

"Do you want me to go over there and play matchmaker for you?" Kim stood up, "besides his fine friend to the right of him has been eyeing me since we've been sitting here." Kim pushed her chair back to leave the table.

"No. Please don't." Pam shrieked holding Kim's arm. "Sit down." She pleaded with Kim with her eyes.

Kim sat down. "Okay, I won't go over there to play matchmaker for you, but trust and believe that I will be introducing myself to his friend before either of us leave here." Kim chuckled. She sipped on her bottled water. She put the water down and turned to face Pam. "And when did you become so docile and all, that's Renee's demeanor, not yours." Kim scrunched her eyebrows.

Pam laughed. "What? There's a time and a place for everything. Yes, I am aggressive when it comes to my career and educational goals, but men are a different story. Clearly with my track record, I don't know what I'm doing when it comes to them. I'mma have to sit back and let God author my love story." Pam gave Kim a half-smile.

Kim looked at Pam for a moment gauging her sincerity. "Well I'll leave it alone, for now. Besides, a minute ago, I heard your stomach growl like a monster hiding under a little kid's bed. Let's go get you some food. Maybe that'll perk you up some."

***

On the other side of the parking lot, Vance and the rest of the guys huddled near the barbecue pits.

"Man, I'm so glad you're done with that 'Jesus ain't Lord hogwash'." Darius clowned as he bit into a hotdog. Barbecue sauce dripped from it staining his white shirt.

Anthony pointed and laughed at him. "Haa. I bet you she won't find you attractive now. A grown man needing a bib."

"Whatever, I have choices, I can either get another shirt from my car or I can use the stain and the heat out here as an excuse to go shirtless and expose my sexy physique." Darius started doing body building poses and kissing his triceps.

"Man, sexy physique? You got a keg, not a six pack." Anthony said.

All of the other guys laughed except for Darius.

"Man, whatever. I may not have the rock hard abs I once I had, but I definitely ain't rocking no keg." Darius started to lift his shirt up.

"Nooo." The rest of the guys said at the same time holding their hands up to him in protest.

They didn't bother to protest the truth that Darius always did manage to get whatever woman he decided to give his attention to.

"Getting back to you Vance, it really is a blessing to see how active you've become in such ashort time with the young men at your dad's church since you've been back there."

Vance smiled. "Thanks."

"Yeah, they all have taken a liking to him, especially this young guy Bobby." Marcus smiled thinking on how he knew his father would love to see the work Vance was doing with the young men's ministry.

"Yeah, Bobby really is a great kid." Vance said.

"Yeah, he was never really bad, just out there doing what he felt like he had to do to protect and try and provide for his mother. Mom really loves him, she treats him like he's her grandson. She's spent so much time praying for him and look how God answered her prayers, he redirected you to be a role model for him." Marcus patted his brother on the back. "Now turn that meat over before you burn it."

They all laughed.

"Man, I know what I'm doing." Vance said.

Marcus feigned coughing as he spoke, "no you don't."

Vance's eyebrows furrowed as he looked at Marcus. "What?"

"The man said you don't know what you're doing." Darius stood there staring down Vance.

"Man, y'all tripping. Y'all know I been throwing down on the grill since my college days and y'all have always loved it. So don't start faking like you don't now. If anything, it's gotten better over the years." Vance did a little dance as he turned some hot links over.

The other guys laughed and shook their heads. Vance wiped his hands off on a towel nearby and turned to face them. "What's so funny? Am I missing something?"

"Clearly you are. We're not talking about your cooking skills." Anthony said.

"So then, what?" Vance frowned

Marcus stood up and walked closer to Vance. He put his hand on Vance's shoulder as he spoke to him. "Man, bro, dude, idiot. I was talking about you don't know much because you haven't tried approaching that woman you really care for. What's her name again?"

"Pam."

"See, look how you said her name, all lovey-dovey like." Darius said laughing.

Vance brushed Marcus's hand off his shoulder. "If that's what y'all thinking, then you better bump heads and change your thoughts because that ain't gonna happen. And I haven't talked to y'all much about her, so why would y'all even bring her up?"

"A man knows when another man is having woman troubles." Darius stated matter-of-factly.

"True." Anthony said.

They all laughed.

"She's the last woman you mentioned to us and the way you talked about her let us know you were really feeling her." Marcus said. "Plus we see how you keep looking at the woman in the purple dress with those sad puppy dog eyes of yours every chance you get. Is that Pam?"

"Yeah, but whatever. All I know, it's only so many times a woman can push a man away before he stops trying to win her over." Vance turned towards the grill to get the remaining meat from it. He closed the lid to let the fire start to die out.

"Yeah man that's true, but the road for y'all wasn't paved so clear. I mean much of the time you chased after her y'all wasn't even of the same faith, so I can understand why she wasn't willing to give you a shot." Anthony guzzled down the rest of his pop.

"True, even I know that I ain't supposed to deal with women who don't believe in God." Darius laughed.

"It's a lot of stuff you're not supposed to be doing since you believe in God." Marcus shook his head.

Darius looked at Marcus. He wanted to stick his middle finger up at him but not wanting to disrespect the women around he dismissed the thought. "Man whatever, this convo ain't about me, we talking 'bout Vance right now." Darius wiped sweat from his eyebrows.

The other guys laughed.

Darius continued talking, "and then the other times you were on her heels, you said it yourself, she was dealing with family issues. I say you can't blame her for not wanting you then-"

Marcus interrupted Darius, "but I have a strong feeling that she's the one for you man."

"You don't even know her." Vance laughed.

Darius looked at Marcus with wide-eyes. "How you gon' cut me off man when I'm making poignant points?"

"Uh oh Marcus, wait y'all. When Darius pulls out his MBA vocab, you know it's on." Anthony said.

The guys laughed.

"Fool you crazy, the word 'poignant' isn't indigenous to MBA holders." Vance laughed.

Darius threw his hands up in the air and walked in circles acting as if he were about to battle someone in breakdancing. "Now you done got the wordsmith ready to unleash his vocabulary. I tell you about educated brothers."

The other guys laughed.

"You're right Vance, I don't know her, but I know no other woman has affected you the way she seems to. I was talking to my wife about it the other day." Marcus said.

Vance scrunched his face up at his brother.

Marcus laughed. "Don't act like you don't know I talk to my wife about you. She cares about you as much as I do. She wants to see you find love and start a family too."

Vance began to sulk.

"And when we were talking she brought up a great point." Marcus paused for a dramatic effect.

All of the other guys sat attentively waiting to hear what Marcus's wife had to say.

"What?" Marcus asked laughing at them as he started eating from the plate he had made for himself earlier.

"Would you talk already." Vance nudged Marcus before he took a seat across from him at the table.

The other guys all turned to face inward to the table. Marcus waited until he finished chewing on his spaghetti and wiped any traces of sauce from his mouth before he spoke. "She thinks the reason why you were so drawn to Pam is because of the God in her." He put another fork full of spaghetti in his mouth.

Vance sat silent in his chair with his hands clasped together on his head. He leaned forward resting his forearms on the table and looked to his brother. "So she thinks I was only drawn to Pam so that I could be reintroduced to God? There was never nothing there long-term for us?"

"Yeah, I think you were drawn to the God in her to bring you back to God but I honestly believe she's the one for you and judging by the way her and her friend keeps looking over here, I think she's just as into you," Marcus said.

Vance looked back over his shoulder and locked eyes with Pam as she stood in line waiting to get her food.

Her stare lingered with his for a minute. It was one of sadness but hope at the same time. He held her stare until she had no choice but to turn away to get out the way for the others in line behind her.

"Man, you better make a move. The same way you said it's only so long a man will chase a woman before he realizes he has no chance with her, is the same way a woman will only leave herself open for a man's advances for so long before she realizes he won't be pursuing her." Marcus sat back in his chair.

Of all the food he had cooked and grilled for the day, Vance didn't even have an appetite to eat.

***

"Ms. Robinson, I mean Pam, can I speak with you in private for a second?" Vance asked nervously as he positioned himself next to the table she sat at.

Kim smirked. "Girl, I'll be back, let me go over here and talk with my grade level team."

She grabbed her plate of cake, looked up at Vance and winked, then walked away.

"May I?" Vance motioned to take a seat in front of Pam.

"Sure."

"How are you doing?" Vance asked.

"I'm good." Pam gave Vance a half smile.

"Good. So, how's your mom?"

Pam perked up some at the mention of her mother. "She's doing great."

"That's good to know." Vance looked down at his thumbs as he rotated them in circles around one another.

Pam laughed inwardly at Vance fidgeting in front of her. She decided to speak up. "So, what's up?" She swirled her fork in her spaghetti awaiting his response.

Vance pulled his chair closer to the table. He cleared his throat and wiped his eyebrows clear of sweat. He took a deep breath. "I'll be upfront and honest with you. I have been very attracted to you over this past year. I was hoping that we could be more than colleagues despite our religious beliefs, but you made it *very* clear that would never happen." Vance said staring at Pam.

She became unnerved under his stare and looked down at her plate. She looked up slightly at him. "I did, didn't I?"

He laughed a little. "Yeah, you did, but that's okay. Maybe it was because whatever you have going on with the parent I saw you with in the parking lot the other day."

Pam looked up at Vance with alarm. She wasn't sure how much of her involvement with Steve she would share with him, so she paused searching for the best words to say. "That guy, Steve was in some way a part of the reason why I couldn't give you a chance, but not in the way you think."

Vance's eyebrows raised.

Pam chuckled at Vance's unspoken response.

"My past with him did make me question if I could trust myself to judge whether or not a man was right for me, but when it came to you, it really got down to us to being unequally yoked, not to mention you're my boss."

"Well we're on the same page with God now, so that issue is solved. And as far as me being your boss, if that's the only thing still hindering us from exploring a relationship, well then, you're fired." Vance tried to remain stoic.

Pam stared at him with her eyes bucked and her mouth wide open trying to gauge if he was serious. When he cracked a smile, she threw a napkin at him. "You better had been playing. I love it here." She smiled.

Vance laughed. "I was joking, but seriously, if that's still the only reason you don't want to give us a go, then I can have you transferred to another school in the district where I know the school culture and climate is like ours."

Pam zoned her stare in on Vance. "You will do no such thing." She sat back in her chair pouting as she folded her arms across her chest.

"Forgive me for being so forward, but, but-"

"Just say it." She prodded him.

"You are so sexy pouting right now." Vance held his breath for her response.

Pam paused. "Thank you, but hey, don't be so loud. I don't want anyone else to know that we're attracted to one another." She quickly covered her gaping mouth shocked that she had said that to him.

"Oh, so you're finally admitting that you like me like that?" Vance did the cabbage patch dance in his seat.

"That dance is so old and yes that's one of my hesitations with you. If we are going to see where this thing could go between us, we have to keep it private."

"If? Don't say if, this between us *is* going somewhere." Vance smiled at her. "Straight to the altar." He coughed out the last part of his statement.

"I'm sorry, what did you say?" Pam really didn't understand what he said.

"Oh nothing, you'll find out soon enough."

"Like you have to tell me the whole story behind you surrendering to God and why you left him in the first place?"

"Yup, I'll tell you that on our first date."

"Are you asking me out on a date?"

"Of course." He winked at her. "And if you're so private about us, why does Ms. Williams seem to know about us? And I'm certain you've talked to your other friends about me." Vance snickered.

"Well, they're my girls, my best friends, my sisters, so yes they know about you."

Vance winked.

"What about your friends? Do they know how you feel about me?" Pam looked at him suspiciously out the corner of her eye.

Vance laughed. "Of course they do, so you might as well grab your plate and come over and meet them."

"Okay, I guess I can meet them now. Plus, they can tell me some more stuff I should know about you." Pam winked. "But I'm certain if I go over there, Kim will come over too."

Vance stood as Pam stood up.

"I figured that. I see how close you two are. I must warn you though, my guy Darius has his eye on her."

Pam laughed as she picked up her plate and drink. "Well Vance, if that's him in the white shirt with the barbecue sauce stain on it, then she has her eye on him too, so this should be interesting."

Other Books Available

Sisterhood Chronicles Series
Underneath It All
Discovery
Untold
When It Happens To You
All Things Considered

Forever Friends Series
Catch Me If You Can
It's Complicated

Limelight Series
Hues
Tones
Vision

Standalone Titles
After All Is Said & Done
The Bid Catcher: Distinguished Gentlemen Series

(Best if you read Forever Friends series before reading Sisterhood Chronicles 3)

COMING SOON

The Kissing Game: Love Alive 1

ABOUT THE AUTHOR

Anita Davis is a former elementary teacher born and raised in Chicago. Although she wrote short stories much of her childhood, she didn't unlock and cultivate her passion as a writer until she became a writing teacher for middle school students. The more she had to create sample writings for her students, the more she realized her passion and ability to tell stories in the written form. She decided to hone her craft as a writer by completing her Master of Fine Arts in Creative Writing via National University. She now pursues writing books most of her time in addition to being a flight attendant. Anita seeks to encourage, engage, and entertain her readers.

She is Co-Founder of Book Euphoria, a group of Chicago authors bound by their love of literature. Book Euphoria hosts literary events and they also founded the empowerment movement, Black Girl Passion.

Anita writes contemporary romantic women's fiction and seeks to encourage, engage, and entertain her readers.

authoranitadavis@gmail.com
www.authoranitadavis.com
Facebook: Anita Davis and Author page: Author Anita Davis
Instagram: @authoranitadavis   Twitter: @_AnitaDavis